HIDDEN

PERFECTLY IMPERFECT SERIES

truths

NEVA ALTAJ

This book is dedicated to my readers, who gave so much love to my books and showed such an amazing support to a baby author like me. Thank you for taking a chance on my stories and motivating me to continue writing. I love you guys. <3

Author's Note

Dear reader, there are a few Russian words mentioned in the book, so here are the translations and clarifications:

Pakhan (пахан)—the head of Russian mafia.

Bratva (братва́)—Russian organized crime or Russian mafia.

Lisichka (лиси́чка)—little fox.

Palomita—little dove; a diminutive of "*paloma*" which means "dove".

TRIGGER WARNING

Please be aware that this book contains content that some readers may find disturbing, such as: gore, violence, abuse, and graphic descriptions of torture. Themes of post-traumatic stress disorder (PTSD) and other mental health conditions are also mentioned.

While we all want to believe that love heals all wounds, please keep in mind that this story is a work of fiction. If you're suffering from PTSD or struggling with other mental health issues, help is available. Reach out to your family and friends, a medical doctor, or another trusted professional, such as a counselor or spiritual leader. You are not alone!

HIDDEN

PERFECTLY IMPERFECT SERIES

truths

Prologue

Email Correspondence

Fifteen years ago

From: Felix Allen
To: Captain L. Kruger
Subject: Sergei Belov

Captain,

I feel the need to express my significant concern regarding the newest recruit I have been assigned, Sergei Belov. The Belov boy is extremely intelligent and shows great physical potential. However, I am not sure he is the right choice for our program. He is only fourteen, and that is way too young. Furthermore, his psychological profile doesn't match our requirements. In plain terms, he is a protector. He is also not a naturally violent individual, and I am not sure how wise it is to proceed. I think he should either be reassigned to another unit or returned to the youth correctional facility he was taken from.

Felix Allen
Z.E.R.O. unit
Handler to Sergei Belov

Eleven years ago

From: Felix Allen
To: Captain L. Kruger
Subject: IMPORTANT. Sergei Belov

Captain,

I am aware of your standing with regard to the Belov kid. I am also aware that his overachievement and impeccable training scores over the past few years may lead to a conclusion that he's acclimated well, and that he is ready to be sent on field missions. It is my professional opinion that he is NOT suitable to perform the missions allocated to the Project Z.E.R.O. operation, and I recommend that he be transferred to one of the standard units as soon as possible.

Felix Allen
Z.E.R.O. unit
Handler to Sergei Belov

Eight years ago

From: Felix Allen
To: Captain L. Kruger
Subject: Transfer request notice

Captain,

Sergei Belov has been showing highly concerning behavior since he returned from the Colombia mission in February. I'm enclosing my full report with this email, but to summarize the most important points: violent outbursts, losing connection with reality, and random catatonic episodes.

I wanted to inform you that I have officially requested a transfer for him, as well as a psychiatric evaluation.

What happened down there, Lennox? Why am I denied access to the mission report? Sergei won't tell me, and when I tried asking around, I was told to leave it be or face consequences. I need to know what happened in Colombia because it was obviously a trigger for the change in his behavior.

Felix Allen
Z.E.R.O. unit
Handler to Sergei Belov

Six years ago

From: Felix Allen
To: Captain L. Kruger
Subject: Urgent

I need you to release Sergei Belov from duty. He poses a danger to other people, but mostly to himself. I tried to explain numerous times, but you wouldn't listen. You can't take a normal kid and shape him into your weapon without consequences. Not everyone is fit to be a fucking hitman, Lennox, no matter how young you throw them into training. It's just a matter of time before he'll snap, and when he does, he'll create chaos that you'll have to explain to our superiors.

Felix Allen
Z.E.R.O. unit
Handler to Sergei Belov

Four years ago

From: Captain L. Kruger
To: Felix Allen
Subject: Where is my asset?!

Felix,

I'm expecting you in my office tomorrow morning. I want to know how the fuck you convinced the admiral to release Belov and yourself. And where are you hiding my asset?!

Captain Lennox Kruger
Project Z.E.R.O. Commander

From: Felix Allen
To: Captain L. Kruger
Subject: Re: Where is my asset?!

Fuck you, Lennox.
I hope your pet project comes back to bite you in the ass real soon.

Felix

CHAPTER
one

Three days ago

THERE ARE EXACTLY ELEVEN PIECES OF MEAT AND twenty-three french fries on the plate. I have counted them at least twenty times since Maria brought the food two hours ago. It was harder to resist while the food was still warm, filling my nostrils with its aroma. But even now, my mouth waters and my gut clenches.

The second day was the worst. I thought I would lose my mind, so I started counting the pieces of food and imagined I was eating them. It helped. Somewhat. Maybe it would have been easier if the meat wasn't cut into small pieces, each one taunting me. I could have taken just one, and no one would have noticed. I don't know how I prevailed that day.

I'm on the fifth day of my hunger strike. They bring me food and water three times a day, but I don't touch anything except water. I would rather die of starvation than willingly marry my father's killer.

The door on the other side of the room opens and Maria walks in. We were best friends once. Until she started fucking my father. I wonder when she decided to switch to Diego Rivera—my father's best friend, business partner, and as of five days ago, his killer.

"There is no point in this, Angelina," Maria says and comes to stand before me with her hands on her hips. "You will marry Diego one way or another. Why choose the harder way?"

I cross my arms and lean against the wall. "And why don't you?" I ask. "You are already fucking him. Why stop there?"

"Diego would never marry a servant's daughter. But he will continue fucking me." She gifts me one of her particularly condescending looks. "I doubt he'll want to touch you now, Manny Sandoval's daughter or not. You were never anything special, but now you look half dead."

"You could ask him to let me go and have him all for yourself."

I can't imagine how she stomachs having that pig touch her. Diego is older than my father was, and he stinks. I will always associate the smell of stale sweat and bad cologne with him.

"Oh, I would. Gladly." She smiles. "If I thought it would work. Diego believes that taking over your father's business contracts will go much smoother with the Sandoval princess as his wife. He will wait a day, maybe two more. Then, he'll drag you to the altar. He has been incredibly patient with you, Angelina. You shouldn't test him much longer." She takes the plate with the untouched food and leaves the room, locking the door behind her.

I lie down on my bed and watch the curtains billow on

7

the light evening breeze. I've been feeling dizzy since this morning, so falling asleep is no longer as hard as it was a few days ago. There are also no more tears left.

I still can't believe that my dad is gone. Maybe he wasn't the best father on the planet, but he was *my* father. Work always came first for Manuel Sandoval, which wasn't unusual. No one expected the head of one of the three biggest Mexican cartels to spend a day playing hide-and-seek with his kid, or anything like that, but he loved me in his own way. A sad smile forms on my lips. Manny Sandoval might not have come to my recitals or helped me with homework, but he made sure I knew how to shoot almost as good as any of his men.

Male laughter reaches me from the patio, making me shudder. That lying bastard and his men are still celebrating. It wasn't enough that he killed my father, the man he did business with for more than a decade. Oh, no. He took over his home and his business contracts. And now, he wants to take his daughter as well.

I close my eyes and recall the day when Diego came to our house. Nobody suspected anything because for years he had visited my father at least once a month. When we realized what was happening, it was already too late.

I shouldn't have attacked Diego that day. The only thing it bought me was a blow across the face that made me see stars. When I saw my father's body lying on the floor, with blood pooling on either side, I couldn't think straight. Killing the asshole was the only thing on my mind. Instead of waiting for a better opportunity, I completely disregarded his two soldiers, took one of the decorative swords hanging on the office wall, and lunged at Diego. His men caught me before I even came close to their boss. And laughed. And then they laughed some more when Diego slapped me across the face, almost dislocating my jaw.

I'm amazed he hasn't come to fuck me already. He's probably busy raping the girls he's brought and locked up in the basement before he ships them off to the men who bought them. I wonder if he'll sell me too, or if he'll just kill me when he realizes I'd rather die than have anything to do with him.

I bury my face into the pillow.

The sound of someone's rushed steps wakes me from my sleep. Slowly and without opening my eyes, I reach under the pillow and wrap my hand around the armrest of the chair I disassembled three days ago. I placed my makeshift weapon there for when Diego finally decides to visit me.

"Angelinita!" A hand grabs my shoulder and shakes me. "Wake up. We don't have much time."

"Nana?" I sit up in the bed and squint my eyes at my childhood nanny. "How did you get in?"

"Come on! And be quiet." She grabs my hand and ushers me out of the room.

They've kept me prisoner in my room, and I haven't eaten for five days straight. My feet drag as I try to keep up with my old and frail nana, who practically drags me along the hallway and down two sets of stairs until we reach the kitchen. Diego doesn't post guards inside the house, and the other staff leave around ten. It must be well into the night, then, since we don't run into anyone.

Nana moves me to stand in front of the glass door that leads to the backyard and points with her finger. "See that truck? They're leaving in twenty minutes. Diego is sending drugs to the Italians in Chicago, and he told me to send one of the girls with the cargo as a present." She looks up at me. "You're going instead."

"What? No." I put my hand on her wrinkled cheek while leaning myself on the wall with the other in case my legs give out. "Diego will kill you."

"You are going. I won't let that son of a bitch have you."

"Nana . . ."

"When you get to Chicago, you can stay with some of your American friends from your studies. Diego won't dare cross the border to come after you."

"I don't have any papers or a passport. What will I do when I get there?" I skip mentioning that I don't have that many friends there either. "And the driver will recognize me."

"He probably won't, you look terrible. But we'll make sure, just in case."

She reaches into the drawer, takes out scissors, and starts cutting my shorts and T-shirt in a couple of places. When she's done, there is barely any cloth left to cover my boobs and ass. Just like Diego likes it.

"Now, the hair."

I close my eyes, take a deep breath, and turn my back to her. I don't let the tears fall as Nana shreds my waist-long hair until it barely reaches my shoulders in slightly uneven strands.

"As soon as you reach Chicago, contact Liam O'Neil," she says. "He can help you get the papers and a new passport."

"I don't think that's wise, considering the situation. What if O'Neil tells Diego I'm there?" My father did business with the Irish for the past year, but he was never a fan of their leader. He called Liam O'Neil a "tricky bastard".

10

"You have to risk it. No one else can get you forged documents."

I stare at the floor where black strands of hair lie around my bare feet. It'll grow back . . . if I live to see that happen.

Nana taps me on the shoulder. "Turn around."

When I do, she grabs a flowerpot with her favorite agave plant from the table, takes a handful of soil, and starts smearing the dirt over on my arms and legs. She takes a step back, looks at me, then spreads a little bit of it on my forehead as well.

"Good." She nods.

I look down at myself. My hip bones are protruding, and my stomach looks sunken. I was always on the thin side, but now my body looks like someone sucked every piece of flesh from it, leaving only skin and bones. I definitely resemble the girls Diego locked away in the basement. When I look up, Nana is watching me with tears in her eyes.

"Take this." She grabs a bag that has been hanging on the chair and thrusts it in my hands. "Some food and water. I didn't dare to put money in, in case the driver decides to check it."

I wrap my arm around her, bury my face in the crook of her neck, and inhale the smell of powdery fabric softener and cookies. It reminds me of childhood, summer days, and love. "I can't leave you, Nana."

"No time for that." She sniffs. "Let's go. Head down and don't speak."

Outside, holding on to my upper arm, she drags me toward the truck parked in front of the service building.

"It's about time, Guadalupe," the driver barks and throws his cigarette on the ground. "Get her in the back. We're late."

"You don't want to get near her." Nana pushes me around the driver. "The bitch vomited all over herself. She stinks."

I keep my head down and try not to trip as I jump inside the back of the truck. My legs are trembling from the strain of trying to hold myself upright. I duck behind one of the boxes and turn to look at Nana Guadalupe one last time, but the big, sliding door drops down with a bang before I can catch a glimpse. The dark is complete, and a minute later, the engine roars to life.

Sergei

The phone in my back pocket rings. I send the knife I've been holding in my right hand flying, then reach for the phone and take the call.

"Yes?"

"The Italians' shipment just left Mexico," Roman Petrov, the Bratva's pakhan says from the other side. "I need you to go with Mikhail when the men head out to intercept it tomorrow night."

"Oh? Does this mean I'm allowed in the field again?"

When I joined the Russian Bratva four years ago, I started as a foot soldier, and during these past years, I climbed the ladder to the pakhan's inner circle. I handled the field duties until a year ago when Roman banned me from them.

"No. This will be a one-time deal. Anton is still in hospital, and we're short-handed, or I would never send you."

"Your motivational speeches require serious work." I fling the next knife through the air.

"When you're motivated, the body count tends to climb through the roof, Sergei."

I roll my eyes. "What do you need me to do?"

"Rig their truck and blow the thing. It will have to be while the driver stops to sleep, because our intel says that there's a girl on the truck with the drugs. We need to get her out first. Mikhail will call you later with more details."

"Okay."

"And make sure it's just the truck that gets blown up this time," he barks and cuts the call.

I throw the last of my knives, turn on the lamp, and walk toward the narrow wooden board mounted on the opposite wall to inspect my hits. Two of the knives landed a little below the target. I'm getting rusty. I pull out the knives and stroll back across the room. Focusing on the white line painted horizontally along the wooden board, I turn off the light again.

Twenty minutes later I leave my room and head downstairs to look for Felix.

"Albert!" I shout.

He hates it when I call him that, so I make sure I always do. Serves him right since he decided to play my butler instead of spending his retirement at a sea cottage like he should have done when the military let us leave. He never told me exactly how he managed to get us released from our contracts.

"Albert! Where did you put our C-4 stash?"

"In the pantry!" he yells from somewhere in the kitchen. "The box below the crate with potatoes."

13

I snort. And they say I'm the crazy one. I circle the stairs and open the pantry door. "Where?"

"Eleven o'clock. Watch your head!"

I turn to the left and smack my skull on the golf equipment bag hanging from the ceiling. "Jesus! I told you to keep your crap in the garage!"

"Not enough room," Felix says from behind me. "Why do you need the C-4?"

"Roman needs me to blow up some shit tomorrow."

"Another Italian warehouse?"

"A truck with their drugs this time." I remove the crate with potatoes and reach for the box. "You can't store explosives with food, damn it. I'm taking this to the basement."

"I need the day after tomorrow off," he calls after me. "I'm taking Marlene to the movies."

I stop and look him in the eyes. "You don't work for me. You're a pest I've been trying to get rid of for years—one who won't leave. I live for the day you finally move in with Marlene and get off my back."

"Oh, I won't be moving in with her anytime soon. It's too early."

"You're seventy-one! If you wait much longer, the only place you'll be moving into is the fucking cemetery!"

"Nah." He waves his hand as if it's nothing. "My family is known for longevity."

I close my eyes and sigh. "I'm doing okay. You don't have to babysit me. Marlene is a nice lady. Go live your life."

The carefree mask vanishes from Felix's face as he grinds his teeth and fixes me with his gaze. "You are far from okay, and we both know it."

"Even if that's true, I'm not your responsibility anymore. Leave. Let me deal with my shit alone."

"You sleep through the night, the whole night, three days in a row and I'll leave. Until that happens, I'm staying put." He turns and heads to the kitchen, then throws over his shoulder, "Mimi knocked over the lamp in the living room. There's glass everywhere."

"You didn't clean it?"

"I don't work for you, remember? If you need me, I'll be in the kitchen. We're having fish for lunch."

Chapter Two

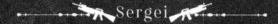
Sergei

I'M LYING UNDER THE TRUCK, SETTING UP THE SECOND pack of explosives when Mikhail curses somewhere on the other side.

"Sergei! Are you done?"

"Just one more," I say.

"You put enough of that shit to blow up the whole damn street. Leave it and come here. The door is jammed."

I roll out from under the truck and walk to the back where Mikhail is holding the cargo door open with the crowbar.

"Just keep it there, I'll get the girl," I say, turn on my phone's flashlight, and jump up into the truck.

I walk around the boxes, moving them around as I pass, but I can't see the girl.

"Is she there?" Mikhail asks.

"I can't find her. Are you sure she's . . ."

There is something in the corner, but I can't see what it is. I round a pile of crates and direct my light down. "Oh, fuck!"

I move the boxes so I can get closer and crouch in front of

a curled-up body. The girl's face is hidden under her arm. Her extremely thin arm. A night eight years ago surges through my mind, and I close my eyes trying to suppress the images of another girl, her thin body covered in dirt. The flashback passes.

I reach out to check the girl's pulse, absolutely positive I won't find one when she stirs and removes her arm. Two impossibly dark eyes, so dark they look black in the light from my phone, stare at me.

"It's okay," I whisper. "You're safe."

The girl blinks, then coughs, and those magnificent eyes roll up and flutter closed. She's fainted. I prop the phone on the box next to me, the light shining on her, and slide my arms under her frail body. My throat tightens as I lift her.

Dear God, she can't weigh more than ninety pounds.

"Sergei?" Mikhail calls from the door.

"I've got her! Shit, she's in bad shape." I take my phone and, using it to light the way through the maze of boxes, carry her out. "I've got you," I say into her ear, then look at Mikhail. "Hold that door."

I jump down from the truck and head toward Mikhail's car.

"I'll call Varya and tell her to bring the doc." Mikhail lets the truck door crash back down. "We can meet them at the safe house."

"No," I bark and pull the small body to my chest. "I'm taking her to my place."

"What? Are you crazy?"

I stop and turn toward him. "I said I'm taking her with me."

Mikhail stares at me, then shakes his head. "Whatever. Get her into the car, blow the truck, and let's get out of here."

17

I open the door and duck into the backseat, holding the girl securely in my arms, then bend and try to listen for her breathing. It's shallow, but she's alive. For now.

"Ready?" Mikhail asks from the driver's seat, but I ignore him. "Jesus, Sergei! Get that fucking remote and blow the fucking truck already."

I look up at him, debating if I should clock him upside the head for interrupting me, and decide against it. That wife of his must be crazy in love with him and his grumpy personality. She wouldn't be happy if he came home with a lump on the side of his head and his ear looking like a hamburger.

I probably wouldn't end up in a much better state. Mikhail is one strong motherfucker. I once witnessed him in a fight with three guys his size. It was fun to watch. I don't remember for sure, but I think he was the only one who came out of that fight alive. I wonder how he lost his right eye as his left eye zeros in on me in the rearview mirror. I smirk, reach for the remote in my pocket, and press the button.

The epic boom pierces the night.

Angelina

Dark. Only dark. Suddenly, a strong light blinds me. Hushed words. Then, a big fat nothing for quite some time.

Light. Weightlessness. More hushed words, but I can't decipher their meaning. Glaring light again. Dog barking. Voices. Three male. One female.

Weightlessness again. Water. Warm. On my body, and then in my hair. I sigh and feel myself drifting away. The water disappears, and suddenly I am so, so cold. Shivering. I try opening my eyes but fail. Something soft and warm envelops my body, then weightlessness again. Arms, big and strong, cradling me. Where am I? Who is carrying me? Adrift on the waves. To where?

The rocking stops, but the arms are still there. I'm cold again, trembling once more. The arms tighten around me and pull me into something warm and solid.

Hushed whispering. Female. Then, clipped deep words. Angry. Male. The arms clench, drawing me even closer. A pinch on the back of my hand. A slight pain. More words. Arguing. The language seems vaguely familiar. It's not Spanish. Not English either. The truck was supposed to go to the Italians, but it's not Italian I'm hearing, not even close.

"*Idi na khuy*, Albert!" a deep male voice snaps next to my ear.

My blood runs cold. How the hell did I end up with the Russians? My Russian is basic since I only took one semester, but I know enough to recognize the language.

I try opening my eyes again, but it's even harder than before. Did they drug me? I'm losing consciousness again, and the last things I remember are hushed words next to my ear and a fresh woodsy scent of male cologne. I shouldn't let myself drift while surrounded by these people, but the deep and soothing voice lulls me, and for some reason, the sound makes me feel safe. Sighing, I bury my face into the hard male chest and fall asleep in the arms of the enemy.

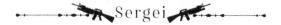

Sergei

I move the sleeping girl so her head rests on my shoulder and rearrange the blanket I wrapped her in. Focusing on her ghostly pale face, I lean back in the recliner. There are big circles around her eyes, and a few wet, unevenly cut strands of hair plastered to her cheek over the faded, yellow bruise. She looks like someone who has gone to hell and back.

"You can't keep her here, my boy," Varya, Roman's housekeeper, says. "She needs medical attention."

"The doc will stay here tonight. You can stay as well if you want." I look up. "She is not going anywhere."

Varya shakes her head and turns to the doc. "How serious is the girl's condition?"

"Dehydration. And the beginnings of pneumonia. I gave her a shot of antibiotics. Give her these pills every day till Tuesday." He hands me a bottle of meds and nods toward the IV bag Varya is holding. "She'll also need another bag of saline tonight."

"Anything else?"

"She will probably be sleeping till morning. When she wakes up, give her water and something to eat, but keep the food light for the first day. In general, she's a healthy woman, and this"—he motions toward the girl in my arms—"is recent. They probably starved her."

My body goes still. "You mean, she didn't have enough food?" I stare at the doctor.

"I mean she either had very little or no food at all during the last five, six days. Maybe more."

A burning sensation spreads through my body, starting from my stomach and then outward until it engulfs me. The room around me dims and transforms into a dark basement, the only light coming from my flashlight. There are crates and pieces of broken furniture scattered around. And bodies. At least ten girls, dirty and thin, lying around. My fault. All my fault. If I got in sooner instead of following orders, I might have saved them. I check their pulse, one by one, even though I know they are all dead. Each has a big red dot at the center of their foreheads. All except the last one. A barely audible moan leaves her lips when I press my finger onto her neck. She opens her eyes to look at me, and the pulse under my finger ceases to beat.

"Sergei?" Varya's voice reaches me, but it sounds distant.

I close my eyes and take a deep breath, trying to block the new wave of images. My left hand starts shaking. Fuck. I grind my teeth and squeeze my eyelids together with all my might.

"Shit. Varya, get away from him. Slowly," Felix barks from somewhere on the right. "Everybody out. Now."

One deep breath. Then another. It doesn't help. It feels like I'm going to explode. I hear people leaving and the door closing, but the sounds are mixed with ringing in my ears. The need to destroy something, anything, overcomes me as rage keeps building and building within.

The girl in my arms stirs and moves her head to the left, burying her face in my neck. Her breath on my skin feels like butterfly wings. The flashback fades. She sighs, then coughs. I open my eyes and look down at her, searching for signs of distress, but she seems okay.

I lean back in the recliner to make her more comfortable, pull the blanket over her bony shoulder, and notice my hand has stopped shaking. Tilting my head back, I stare at the ceiling and listen to her breathing, then I try to sync my much faster breaths with hers. The girl's body twitches, and she coughs again.

"It's okay. You're safe," I whisper and tighten my arms around her.

She mumbles something I can't decipher and places her hand on my chest, just above my heart. So small. And so damn thin. I could probably circle both of her wrists between my thumb and forefinger. I reach out and press my palm to the side of her neck, feeling the beat of her pulse under my fingers. It's strong. She'll pull through. The pressure that has been building inside of me slowly recedes.

Gazing at her face again, I tuck the wet strands of her hair behind her ear and regard her. Even starved nearly to death, she is beautiful. But, it's not her beauty that attracts my attention. There is something in the lines of her face that seems familiar. I have an impeccable memory, and I am one hundred percent certain that I haven't met her before, at least not in person. Still . . . I cock my head to the side, examining her black eyebrows, pert nose, and full lips. Trying to imagine how she looked before she was starved and spent three days on that truck. As if she feels my stare, she stirs, and for a fleeting second her eyes open and her unfocused dark gaze meets mine. And I remember.

CHAPTER Three

SOMETHING WET LANDS ON THE BACK OF MY HAND and rolls down between my thumb and forefinger. Panting. Hot breath blows into my face. I open my eyes, blink, and instantly go stone-still. I try to control the rising panic as I stare past a long snout into two dark eyes that watch me with interest. As slowly as possible, I sit up and crawl to the far side of the bed until my back hits the wall, keeping the beast in my sight. I have no issues where dogs are concerned, but the thing looking at me is closer in size to a small pony than to an ordinary dog.

The animal cocks its head, then lays down on the floor and closes its eyes. A few moments later, a sound of deep snoring reaches me. I exhale and look around at my surroundings.

I'm in someone's massive bedroom. In addition to the bed, there's a big wooden armoire, and a floor-to-ceiling bookcase with two recliners and a standing lamp before it. A leather jacket and motorcycle helmet rest casually on one of the recliners. The room has two doors, probably a bathroom and the exit. And there's a strange fixture—a thick wooden board with a white stripe painted horizontally. I blink several times and focus on the door next to the weird decoration. I have to get out of here.

I am pretty sure I somehow ended up with one of the Russian Bratva's soldiers. No one else would have intercepted the drug shipment. Saying that my father wasn't on the best of terms with the Russians would be an understatement. If anyone here finds out who I am, and that Diego is looking for me, they will probably hand me over to that bastard.

I need to leave. Now.

However, before I can try getting out of here, I need to go to the bathroom, because my bladder feels like it's going to burst at any second. I scoot toward the edge of the bed, as far as possible from the sleeping Cerberus on the floor. The moment my feet touch the ground, the dog's head snaps up. I wait for it to attack, but it just keeps watching me from its spot at the side of the bed. Slowly, I stand up, and my vision blurs. When the dizziness passes, I carefully head toward the door on the right, supporting myself on the armoire. My legs are shaking, and the room seems to tilt before me, but I some-how manage to get to the door and grab the handle.

The dog issues a low grumble, not quite a growl, but a warning for sure. I look over my shoulder, and it points its snout to the other door. I inch along the wall to the other door and reach for the doorknob, keeping an eye on the dog. It lays its head down as soon as my hand touches the handle. Strange. I open the door, and sure enough, it's the bathroom.

After emptying my screaming bladder, I approach the sink and stare at my reflection. The first thing I notice is that I'm clean. There are no dirt splotches on my skin, and my hair looks washed. Someone bathed me. They also put clothes on me. I vaguely noticed it as soon as I woke up, but I didn't pay attention to what I was wearing then. It's female clothes, pink shorts and a white T-shirt with a cartoon character on the front. The shorts fit, but the shirt is a little tight over my breasts. Looks like the only fat left in my body is in my boobs.

I splash some water over my face, drink a bit directly from the tap, and start opening the cabinets. I'd kill for a toothbrush because my mouth feels like sandpaper. It must be my lucky day. I find a box with two unused ones under the sink. When I'm done brushing my teeth, I leave the bathroom and head to the other door, but the moment I take a second step in that direction, I hear deep growling. I stop, and the growling ceases. Great. I should have expected that. But now what?

There are a few paces to the exit, but only half that between me and the dog. I wait a couple more minutes, rooted to the spot, then take another step, faster this time. The beast barks and lunges toward me. I cover my face with my hands and scream.

There is a sound of running, and the door opens. I don't dare remove my hands from my face, still expecting the dog to attack.

"Mimi!" a deep voice from somewhere in front of me commands. "*Idi syuda.*"

Mimi? Who in their right mind would name that thing Mimi? I separate my fingers and squint through them to take a glimpse at the owner of the booming voice. When I do, I immediately stumble several steps backward.

I'm not easily intimidated by men. Growing up in a drug cartel compound, I had hard-looking men around me since I was a little girl. But this . . . this man would intimidate anyone.

The guy standing at the door is well over six feet tall and heavily muscled. However, he is not bulky like one would get by pumping weights in the gym and taking supplements. His body must have been honed to perfection over years. Every muscle is perfectly defined and fully on display since he's only wearing faded jeans. And as far as I can tell, he's also fully covered in ink. Both of his arms up to his wrists, torso—all the way up to his collarbones, and, based on the black shapes I can see on his shoulders, his tattoos must continue over his back as well.

I let my gaze travel upward to his face, which is set in sharp lines. His hair is pale blond, creating such a strange combination with his inked skin. But the most intriguing feature is his eyes—glacier blue, clear and piercing—that watch me without blinking.

The scary Russian takes a step toward me. I yelp and take two backward.

"It's okay. I am not going to hurt you," he says in English and raises his hands in front of himself. "What's your name?"

How much should I tell him? He doesn't know who I am, thank God. I've been pretty low-key in my father's business, so it's not like I expected anyone from the Russian Bratva to recognize me. I need to keep it that way. Shit. I should have thought about this and prepared a story.

"*¿Cómo te llamas?*" he asks again, but I keep my lips shut.

I need some time to think, so I look down at the dog he's holding by the collar and pretend to focus on it.

"*Comment tu t'appelles?*"

French? How many languages does this guy speak? I will have to give him an answer soon. Should I give my real name?

It's not rare and rather universal, better to go with the truth than to forget which name I give him.

I decide on English. "It's Angelina." Since I finished high school and attended college in the US, I don't have an accent. And it's safer.

The trembling in my legs is getting worse, and I'm slightly lightheaded again, so I put my hand on the wall and close my eyes, hoping I won't faint. The food Nana gave me—some fruit and a few sandwiches—helped me regain some of my strength, but I ate the last of it yesterday morning.

I feel an arm around my waist and my eyes snap open.

"Back to bed," the Russian says into my ear, places his other arm under my legs and lifts, carrying me toward the bed.

It feels familiar, his closeness. I don't remember much of what happened in the last twenty-four hours, but I do remember feeling strong arms taking me out of that truck, and again later. I lean my head on his shoulder, closer to his neck. Déjà vu. I close my eyes, and inhale his scent, something woodsy and fresh. Familiar. I know this smell from last night. I was delirious and unaware of what was happening around me, but I remember falling asleep to this. Is he the one who found me?

We reach the bed, but he doesn't put me down right away. Instead, he just watches me. His face is only a few inches from mine. He doesn't seem so scary up close without all that ink in view. In fact, he is rather handsome with those sharp cheekbones and pale eyes. The only imperfect thing on his face is his nose, which is slightly crooked as if it had been broken repeatedly. It's strange how being pressed to his naked chest like this doesn't bother me.

"Do you know where you are and how you got here, Angelina?" he asks and lowers me down onto the bed.

His question instantly shakes me out of my daydream. I move my gaze to the dog lying in the middle of the room, snoring. No way am I telling him the truth, but I do need a believable story. One which will convince him that I'm a nobody so he will let me go.

"I was traveling," I say, not removing my gaze from the dog. "Backpacking. I got kidnapped outside of Mexico City last week." There. That sounds believable. Most of the girls Diego had in the basement came to him that way.

"Alone?"

"Yes." I nod.

"And what happened then?"

"They put me into that truck. I don't know where they were taking me before you found me."

There is a short silence, then he continues, "You're in Chicago. Where are you from?"

"Atlanta."

"Do you have family in Atlanta?"

"Yes." I nod. "My mom and dad live there."

"Okay. I'm going to bring you something to eat, and then you can call your parents. Sound good?"

I look up and find him watching me with narrowed eyes.

"Yes, please," I say.

He turns to leave. Just as I thought, his back is also covered in tattoos. He didn't give me his name. It shouldn't matter because I will be gone shortly anyway, but I want to know. "What's your name?"

"Sergei. Sergei Belov." He throws the words over his shoulder and is gone in the next moment.

I stare at the door he closed while panic starts building in my stomach. Shiiiit. Of all the people that could have found me . . .

The Russians were already doing business with Mendoza and Rivera—the heads of the other two cartels—when they approached my father last year with an offer to collaborate. The Bratva wanted an in with the Sandoval cartel as well. My father turned them down, and then partnered with the Irish, who are the Russians' main competitors.

I remember that day very well. I had just returned from the US and was waiting for my father to come back from the meeting with the Russians. He barged into the house, yelling and cursing. I had never seen my father yell so much. When I asked what happened, he said that it was no wonder the Russians get along well with Mendoza because they were all deranged. He didn't elaborate, but later that day, I heard the guards talking about how the Russian who came to a meeting was batshit crazy. The guy sent all four of my father's body-guards to the hospital when they tried to disarm him before letting him speak with my father.

That Russian was Sergei Belov.

I have to get out of here as soon as possible.

Sergei

I take the pot of soup Felix prepared, pour a healthy amount into a bowl, and head toward the fridge, dialing Roman along the way.

"The girl woke up." I reach for the bottle of juice. Doc said she needs to take in some sugar.

"What did she say?"

"Her name is Angelina. Didn't offer last name. She was traveling when Diego's men bagged her and put her on that truck. Says she's from Atlanta and has family there."

"Sounds like something Rivera would do."

"Yeah." I nod and reach for the glass. "Except it's all bullshit."

"You think she's lying?"

"About everything except her name."

"Why would she lie?"

"Because her name is Angelina Sofia Sandoval," I say. "She's Manny Sandoval's daughter, Roman."

"You're shitting me."

"Nope. I have her photo in my folder on Manny from last year. I didn't recognize her right away. Her hair is shorter now, and the photo was old, but it's her."

A stream of curses comes from the other end of the line. "What the fuck was she doing hidden in the Italians' shipment? Did she know the truck was going to be delivered to the Albanians?"

"No clue." I shrug, take the platter with the soup and the juice, and head toward the stairs.

"Let her stay there for now, and don't let her out of your sight until we find out what's going on. I need to focus on the Italians now. Mikhail should be here any moment. We'll handle the cartel princess issue after the situation with Bruno Scardoni blows over."

"Okay." I head upstairs. "But you should know one thing. I'm keeping her, Roman."

"What? You are not keeping her. She's not a fucking stray you can just claim as yours."

"Of course, I can."

"Jesus Christ!" There is a labored sigh on the other side. I can imagine his reaction like he's here in front of me, pressing the bridge of his nose and shaking his head. "You know, I don't have the energy to deal with your fucked-up view of reality at this moment. Call me if she says anything."

"Sure," I lie. I have no intention of sharing anything Angelina-related with him because I plan on dealing with my little liar myself.

Angelina

I take another spoonful of soup and shoot a look at Sergei. He watched me the whole time I ate the first bowl, which took less than two minutes. Then, he went downstairs and brought more. I'm on the third bowl now, and he still hasn't said a thing. He just sits in the recliner near the bookshelf and keeps his vulture-like gaze on me.

Could he be onto me? If he is, he probably would have confronted me already, so I guess I'm good.

He said he'll let me call my parents after I finish with the food, and since they are both dead, I plan to call Regina, a friend from college. I have no clothes, no phone, and no documents. I need money so I can buy the essentials and get myself setup in a motel for a few days. From there, I'll be able to contact O'Neil to help me with the documents, because without those I can't access my accounts. I don't plan on going back to Mexico, but I need to get Nana Guadalupe out of there, too.

I put the platter with the empty bowl on the nightstand, drink the juice, then look up at Sergei. He grabbed some clothes from the armoire before he went to get me more soup and put on a white shirt before returning. It looks good on him, and with his tats covered, he looks less harsh.

"Can I borrow your phone to call my parents now?"

"Of course." He takes the phone from his pocket and throws it to me.

I catch it, type Regina's number, and pray to God she answers.

"Yes?"

"Hey, Mom. It's me," I say, "Angelina."

"Mom?" She giggles. "Have you been drinking?"

"I'm good," I say, ignoring her question. "Yes, the trip was great. I'm in Chicago now."

"Chicago? You said you were staying home for at least two weeks. What are you doing in Chicago?"

"Yeah, I'm with some friends. Listen, I got robbed. They took my money and my documents. I remembered Aunt Liliana lives here, could you send her some money for me?"

"Aunt? You mean my sister?" A few seconds of silence pass on the other side. "What's happening? Are you in danger?"

"Perfect. I'll drop by her place later today. Thanks, Mom. Say hi to Dad."

I cut the call and throw the phone back to Sergei, who is lying back in the recliner, watching me with a barely visible smirk.

"You got robbed?" He raises an eyebrow.

"Yeah, I . . . well, I couldn't tell her I've been kidnapped. She would die of worry. I'll tell her everything when I get home."

"You seem to be very composed for someone who just went through a traumatic experience. Do you get kidnapped often?"

No, I wouldn't say often. Only twice so far, but I don't plan on sharing that detail. Maybe I should have cried, but well, that ship has sailed. "I . . . I'm very good at functioning under pressure."

He smiles. "Indeed."

"Listen," I continue, "I'm really grateful for you guys getting me out of that truck and saving me, but I should be on my merry way. My mom will send me some money, so I'll compensate you for the food and the clothes. I'll just leave now. Sounds good?"

Sergei stands up from his spot, walks toward the bed where I'm sitting, and crouches in front of me. Cocking his head to the side, he regards me and shakes his head, smiling. "You are a terrible liar."

My eyes widen. "Excuse me?"

"You're excused." He nods, then reaches with his hand over and takes my chin between his fingers. "Now, the truth, please."

I take a deep breath and stare at those pale blue eyes which are glued to mine, while his thumb moves along the line of my jaw. The skin of his hand is rough but his touch is so light that I barely register it. His finger reaches the side of my jaw, just over the almost-faded bruise and stops there.

"Who hit you, Angelina?"

I blink. It's hard to focus on anything else when he's so close, but I somehow manage to collect myself. "I fell."

"You fell." He nods and moves his gaze to where his finger is, still next to the bruise. "On someone's fist, maybe?"

33

"No. I tripped. Over one of the boxes in the truck."

His eyes find mine again and I swear my heart skips a beat. "Do you know how much time is needed for a bruise to get that nice yellowish-green color, Angelina?"

"Two days?" I mutter. I never actually thought about that.

"Five to ten days." He leans forward so that his face is right in front of mine, "Tell me the truth."

"I just told you." I whisper "I'm not lying."

"Are you sure?"

"Yes."

"Okay then." His fingers release my chin. Sergei straightens and heads to the door. "The windows are locked and connected to the alarm. Please don't try breaking them," he says. "Mimi is a military-trained dog, and she will be in front of the door the whole time, so don't tire yourself trying to escape, because you're staying here until you start telling me the truth. I'll come to take you downstairs for lunch."

With those words, he leaves the room and closes the door.

Shit.

I spend almost an hour sitting in bed, trying to understand where I fucked up. Except for the bruise thing, my story was solid. I tried to keep it as close as possible to the truth to make it more realistic. How the hell did he catch me? The bigger problem is, I have no idea how much he knows.

Everybody has heard of Sergei Belov, the Bratva's negotiator in all drug-related business. He came to Mexico quite often. What if he recognized me from one of his visits? I don't see how he would, though. I didn't go to Mexico often enough for our paths to cross. And I would have remembered seeing him.

I've always avoided cartel gatherings and parties because those usually ended up devolving into orgies or with someone getting shot. Or both. I preferred reading in the garden or hanging with Nana in the kitchens. Dad liked to say that I was antisocial. I wasn't. I'm not. I've just always been . . . socially awkward.

Maybe Sergei just overheard Regina giggling while we were talking and called me out on pretending to speak with my mom? Still, it would be best to get out of here ASAP. Just in case.

I stand up from the bed, walk across the room and open the door just a crack. Mimi, the Cerberus, is sleeping on the floor just across the threshold, but her head snaps up as soon as she hears the door. Great. I shut it and head toward the windows. Both locked. Now what?

I'm still debating what I should try next when I hear steps approaching, fast. In the next moment, the door to the room bursts open and Sergei barges in. He doesn't pay attention to me, just grabs the helmet and the leather jacket off the recliner and runs out. Shortly after, I hear an engine roar to life outside. I rush to the window just in time to see him turning his huge sports bike onto the street at an insane speed. Less than five seconds later he's out of sight. I rush to the door in hopes that the dog left its guard spot, but no. She's still there. Damn it.

Approximately two hours later, there's a knock at the door and a gray-haired man with glasses comes in, carrying a platter of food. He's in his late sixties or early seventies, has a nicely trimmed beard, and wears a pale-blue shirt with navy slacks.

"Change of plans," he says, approaching the bed. "Sergei had to leave, so you are getting a room service."

He places the platter on the nightstand, turns, and offers me his hand. "I'm Felix."

I grab his fingers. "Please, let me get out of here. Please! Just hold the dog and I'll be gone in a second."

"I'm sorry." He places his other hand over mine. "I can't do that. And even if I could, Mimi wouldn't let you leave this room. She listens only to Sergei's commands."

"Please!"

"You have no money. You don't even have shoes. And you spent the night in delirium because of starvation," he says softly. "You'd faint before reaching the next block."

I let go of his hand and move back. It wasn't like I expected him to help me escape, but I had to try.

"When is Sergei getting back?" I ask. I will have to reason with him, obviously.

"I don't know. But I'll let him know you want to speak with him when he does." He nods toward the platter. "The doc said you should eat only light food for the first day, so I've prepared you risotto with vegetables and some salad. There is also more of the soup. Sergei said you liked it."

"Are you the cook here?"

He doesn't look like a cook. He looks like an accountant.

"The cook. Gardener, as well. And as Sergei likes to call it, a butler." He smiles. "I will leave you to eat now, but I'll come back later to give you your antibiotics and will bring dinner. If you need anything, just open the door and shout. I'll be downstairs."

Sergei

I park the bike in front of the hospital entrance, barge inside, and head toward the information desk.

"Hallway C?" I bark at the guy behind the desk.

"Can you tell me who you are looking for, sir? I need to . . ."

I grab his wrist, pull him toward me, and get in his face. "Hallway. C."

"First floor," he chokes out. "Turn left when you exit the elevator."

I let go of the guy's hand and dash toward the elevator.

"Where is the grumpy bastard?" I ask the moment I round the corner and find Roman standing there. Mikhail's wife is sitting in one of the chairs down the hall, with her legs crossed under her and her head leaning against the wall.

"In the OR," Roman says.

"How bad?"

"Nicked lung."

I squeeze my teeth. "Will he live?"

"I don't know, Sergei." He sighs and passes his hand through his hair. "Go home. I'll let you know the moment I have any info."

"Who shot him?"

"Bruno Scardoni."

"Is the asshole dead?"

"Yes."

Fuck. "If anyone else was involved, I want the list. I'm free this weekend."

"Free for what?"

"To behead each and every one of them." I bite out and turn on my heel, intending to head back home. Instead, I end up riding around the city until well into the night.

CHAPTER
four

I AM NOT SURE WHAT WAKES ME, BUT THE MOMENT I open my eyes, I know I'm not alone in the room. The digital clock on the nightstand shows two a.m. I sit up in the bed and look around the room. I don't notice him at first because he blends well into the darkness. The only thing that gives him away is his hair, caught in the moonlight coming through the window.

"I'm sorry if I woke you," Sergei says from his spot in the recliner.

I doubt it was him who woke me. He is sitting so still that if I didn't know where to look, I wouldn't have noticed him.

"Can't sleep?" I ask.

"No."

He seems relaxed, but there is something in the tone of his voice that seems . . . wrong somehow.

"Why?"

"Too much shit over the past couple of days."

"You should let me go then. One less thing for you to worry about."

"I will. When you tell me the truth."

I blink. "What truth?"

"Why were you on the truck full of drugs that was sent to the Albanians, and why were you starved half to death when we found you?" he asks casually. "We can start with why you lied to me in the first place, Miss Sandoval."

Oh, fuck. I shut my eyes, trying to subdue the rise of panic. He knows who I am, but it doesn't seem like he is aware that Diego is looking for me, so not all is lost. "How do you know who I am? We've never met."

"The Bratva always does thorough research of all our potential partners. Including their family members. There is no point in lying anymore."

I open my eyes and find him watching me. "So, now what?"

"Now you tell me what you were doing on that truck."

I look away. No chance in hell I can tell him the truth. The Bratva does business with Diego, so they will send me back the moment they hear he's looking for me. I'm not risking it.

"It was personal. It shouldn't concern you or the Bratva."

"Everything that happens in this city concerns The Bratva. Especially when a cartel princess lands at my feet, seemingly out of nowhere."

"It was you who found me?" I ask.

"Yes." He leans back and tilts his head up, staring at the ceiling. "Mikhail and I went to intercept the shipment. The intel we had said that there will be a girl on the truck, so we got you out before I blew it up."

"You blew up the truck full of drugs? Why not just take it."

"Pakhan wanted to make a statement." He shrugs as if it's completely normal to destroy several million dollars' worth of product just to make a statement.

"A rather expensive statement."

"Yeah. Roman is a fan of theatrics." He looks over at me. "I'll ask Nina to send you more clothes tomorrow."

"Nina?" Is that Sergei's girlfriend? I look down at the T-shirt I'm wearing. The fact that I'm dressed in his girlfriend's clothes doesn't sit well with me.

"Roman's wife," he clarifies.

"Oh. Pass her my thanks." I'm glad it's not his girlfriend's stuff. "I need you to let me go, Sergei. Please."

"Sure. As soon as you tell me what I need to know."

I press my lips together and lie back down, covering myself with the blanket to my chin.

"Nothing to share?"

"Nope," I mumble.

"When that changes, let me know, and we will discuss your freedom."

I regard him for a long time as he keeps sitting there, staring at the ceiling in silence, his body completely still. I've heard stories about him. My father's men loved to gossip, especially when they got drunk. From what they said, I got the impression that Sergei Belov was some kind of crazed killer, going around and offing people for no reason. Now I've met him, however, that image doesn't seem accurate. He doesn't come across as crazy to me. In fact, he acts like a pretty normal guy.

Maybe I could try seducing him, and then get away when

his guard is down. Yeah, right. I almost snicker out loud at the thought of Angelina Sandoval, a book nerd, and local weirdo who's slept with exactly one man in her twenty-two years, becoming a queen of seduction. He would laugh at me if I tried.

I let my eyes travel over his body, noticing the way his wide chest and shoulders strain the material of the black T-shirt he's wearing, and stop my inspection at his forearms. Thick, strong, and corded with perfectly shaped muscles. Some women are attracted to a man's hair or mouth. I've always been a forearms girl.

I yawn. Does he expect me to go to sleep with him lurking there? I can normally crash in the weirdest of places. In fact, I once fell asleep at a bar, leaning on Regina's shoulder as some guy tried to convince her to go out with him. But I don't think I can sleep while a stranger, whom I consider a threat, is sitting in the same room. What if he tries something? Although, there were enough opportunities for him to do so while I was passed out that first night, and he didn't.

My eyelids are getting heavy, so I decide to close them, but only for a moment. Because there is no way I will let myself actually sleep with . . .

The ringing of a phone wakes me. I actually managed to fall asleep while the Bratva's soldier was in the same room. People go to therapy when they have trouble sleeping, but it looks like I need help knowing when not to fall asleep. It's still partially dark outside, with dawn fast approaching. I turn to look at the recliner and find Sergei still sitting there, holding the phone to his ear. He listens to the person on the other end, and his body suddenly goes rigid, the expression on his face changing from slightly tense to volatile. He doesn't say anything, just lowers the phone and stares at it like he wants to smash it.

"Bad news?" I mumble.

He doesn't reply, just keeps his eyes on the phone with such malice that I wonder if the thing will combust from the intensity of his stare.

I'm not sure what's going on, but it's clear something's happened and it isn't good. It shouldn't matter to me. After all, the guy is keeping me a prisoner in his home indefinitely unless I spill my secrets. But he did save my life. I would probably be dead if he didn't find me, or perhaps worse off if it was someone else.

I should just go back to sleep, but I can't. So, against my better judgment, I get out of bed and slowly walk toward the recliner until I'm standing just in front of him.

"Are you okay?" I ask.

Nothing.

"Sergei?"

Still nothing. He just keeps staring at the phone. I reach out and poke him on his shoulder with the tip of my finger.

His head snaps up, and I start registering the things I missed from a distance. The way he grinds his jaw, the slight shaking of his left hand, and the sound of his breathing— which is a bit faster than normal. But most of all, I am taken aback by his eyes, which are unfocused like he is looking through me.

"Yes?" he asks, his voice sounding . . . detached somehow.

"Did something happen?"

He closes his eyes for a second and takes a deep breath. "Go back to bed. I'll leave."

There is something wrong. I just can't pinpoint what. He seems angry and agitated, but trying to keep it subdued. Other than those little tells, he looks perfectly composed.

He's right. I should go back to bed. What's going on with him is not my problem. I shouldn't care. So, why do I? I focus on his eyes again. Yes, the look in them is really strange.

"Are you meditating or something?" I ask.

He blinks, and I might be wrong because it's still rather dark in the room, but his eyes seem more focused now.

"I am not fucking meditating." He shakes his head. "I just got an update on my friend who was shot yesterday. The one who was with me when we found you. Mikhail."

"Oh." That's probably why he stormed out of the house yesterday morning. "How is he?"

"Bad."

"Will he pull through?"

"They just took him to surgery again. He has internal bleeding."

"Are you two close?" I place my hand on his left one and brush it slightly. His eyes are now honed in on me, and the shaking of the hand beneath mine seems to stop.

"Not really," he says. "But I'll kill him if he dies."

I feel the corners of my lips curl up slightly. He's coming back from wherever he went earlier. "In that case, he'll probably be sure to stay alive."

Without breaking our eye contact, Sergei slides his hand from beneath mine and wraps his fingers around my wrist.

"Who starved you?" he asks leaning toward me.

"I did," I say. "I was on a hunger strike."

"Why?"

I bend my head slightly so our noses almost touch and stare into those light eyes. "I can't tell you."

His lips widen. "I will find out, lisichka."

"Lisichka?" I raise an eyebrow. I don't know that word.

"Little fox." He takes my chin between his fingers. "Appropriate, don't you think?"

"Not really."

He smiles, shakes his head, and gets up from the recliner. I forgot just how tall he is.

"Yes, I think it's perfect." He brushes my chin with his thumb, then turns and heads toward the door. "Go back to sleep, my little liar."

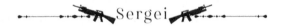

Sergei

Roman calls around noon to let me know Mikhail is out of surgery, and that he should be okay. I pass out on the living room couch shortly afterward. I'm rarely able to sleep during the day, but my brain finally got the memo from my body, which was operating on only a couple of hours of sleep in the last three days. When I wake up, it's already close to four.

"You need to let that girl out of your room. She'll go moldy there," Felix says, passing me by, and hits me with a kitchen rag on my shoulder. "And if you plan on keeping her here, you'll need to get her some clothes. Other than Nina's. And shoes."

"Shit." I sit up and rake my hand through my hair. "Where can I get female clothes?"

"In one of those things they call shops. You can find many inside the big buildings known as malls."

"Such a comedian." I stand up. "How about you go buy some stuff for her?"

"Oh no. She's your prisoner, so you're the one who should dress her and feed her. And I'm already doing the feeding part."

"All right, fine. I'll go right away. I have a meeting with Shevchenko later."

"I thought Shevchenko said he doesn't want to talk business with you anymore. Since you tried to chop off his hand and all."

"He's overreacting," I throw out over my shoulder while looking for my helmet.

"So, you didn't try to cut off his hand?"

"Of course, I did." I shift through the throw that's been haphazardly draped over the couch. "Did you take lunch to Angelina?"

"Nope. I will go get her and give her lunch in the kitchen. She needs to stretch her legs. But you need to call Mimi off so she can come out of the room."

"Make sure she doesn't get away." I whistle for my watchdog, and Mimi comes padding down the stairs. "And don't forget to get me the info I asked for. I need everything you can find on her." I look around the room. "Where the fuck is my helmet?"

"Dining room," Felix says and continues dusting the TV.

"Why are you doing that? It's Marlene's job. Where is she?"

"She's mad because I canceled our date since I had to play the jailer. She told me she's taking the rest of the week off."

"Marlene is my housekeeper. She can't tell you she's taking a week off."

He turns toward me with his hands on his hips and fixes me with his gaze. "I'm getting the job done, so it doesn't matter, does it?"

"Works for me." I raise my hands in defense. "I'm off."

I stop in the middle of the store and turn around, looking over the mile-long racks of female clothes. Shit. Where do I start?

"Need any help?" a store attendant asks, coming to stand next to me.

"Yes. Please."

"Okay." She laughs. "What do you need? A present?"

"I need everything," I say.

"Everything?"

"Yeah. A friend is staying with me, and she lost her luggage. She needs everything."

"No problem. What size?"

I stare at the lady, who probably thinks I'm an idiot. "A little over five feet or so. Around ninety pounds. Does that help?"

"Shoes as well?"

"Yes. I'll have to ask the size for that."

"Sure. Do you want to pick, or do you want me to do that for you?"

I look over at all the racks and shudder. "You pick. Jeans, T-shirts, a jacket. Casual stuff."

"Okay. How many of each?"

"Let's say for a month."

"Socks, underwear? I'll need the bra size."

"Hm. Medium?"

She laughs and shakes her head. "Let's make it sports bras. Those are stretchy."

"Yup, that would work."

"Perfect. I'll start collecting your things. You can wait there, or you can go to the store next door and get her some cosmetics if she needs any."

"I'll do that. Please make sure you pick the good stuff. No budget limit."

I shoot Felix a message, asking about Angelina's shoe size, and head into the neighboring shop. When I tell the attendant what I need, she starts asking me questions about skin and hair type, as if I'm supposed to know that crap. So I just tell her to give me one of everything.

Thirty minutes later, I find myself standing next to my bike with dozens of bags in my hands. I should have brought the car, but I didn't think of that. I end up calling a cab to take the bags back to the house and head home.

Angelina

"THIS IS GREAT." I POINT TO THE MEATBALLS ON my plate and stuff another one in my mouth.

"Finally, someone who appreciates what I do around here," Felix grumbles and continues putting away the dishes from the dishwasher.

I take the opportunity to look around. The kitchen is rather big, with a dining table by the window on the left side. The house itself is not that large, though. Two bedrooms on the upper floor, and a huge living room and kitchen on the ground floor. It's a nice place with new, modern furniture, and it looks lived in. One thing I find strange is there are no photos of any kind. Anywhere.

"Do you live here?" I ask.

"In the apartment above the garage."

"Nice." I look over my shoulder at the front door, calculating the distance. Felix seems rather fit, but he's old. I doubt he would be able to stop me if I can catch him unaware. If the door is unlocked, I should be able to slip away.

"Don't," Felix says, and my head snaps back to him.

"What?"

"Mimi will get you before you even reach the door." He nods toward the living room where the dog is sleeping on the floor next to the sofa.

I feign innocence. "I wasn't planning on doing anything."

"Yeah, right." He puts the plate away, turns toward me, and leans on the counter. "Why don't you just tell Sergei what he needs to know, so he'll let you go?"

"I have my reasons." I resume eating. "How's his friend? The one who got shot."

"He'll be okay," Felix says and crosses his arms in front of his chest. "How do you know about Mikhail?"

"Sergei told me last night. Someone called him to say he wasn't doing well. Sergei got upset."

"Upset?"

"Yeah. He kind of zoned out. It was strange." I shrug and reach for the salad. Felix approaches, grabs my chair, and turns it toward him.

"Zoned out . . . how?" He leans over me, and I stare at him. Gone is the grumpy but funny old guy from a few seconds ago, and in his place stands a very serious and visibly alarmed man.

"I don't know. He just sat there really still. His eyes seemed strange—like he was looking at me without really seeing me," I say. "His hand started shaking."

Felix closes his eyes and curses. "And then?"

"I approached him, but it seemed like he didn't register me, so I poked him, and that got his attention."

Felix's eyes snap open. "You . . . poked him?"

50

"Yeah. With my finger. Like this." I touch his shoulder lightly. "It seemed to help. He snapped out of it after a few minutes, called me a little fox, and left."

"And that's it?"

"Yeah, pretty much so. Why?"

Felix doesn't say anything, only watches me for a few seconds. Then, he pulls out the chair next to him, sits down, and leans toward me. He still doesn't speak. Did I do something I shouldn't?

"Is something . . . wrong with Sergei?" I ask.

"Yes," he says finally. "He sometimes processes things differently. And his views on what should be a logical response to a certain situation differ from yours or mine."

I furrow my eyebrows. "How so?"

"Let's say you're waiting in a line to get a coffee, and a man behind you tries to take your wallet. What would you do?"

"I don't know. Whack him on the head with my bag? Call the police?"

"Sergei would snap his neck, get back in the line, and order a cappuccino when his turn comes."

I blink. "He . . . he doesn't seem like a violent person."

"Sergei is not naturally violent. He would never attack anyone under normal circumstances. He would never touch a child. Or a woman, unless she's a threat. If an old woman is crossing a street, he'll approach to help her. If a cat gets stuck in a tree, he'll climb it and rescue the cat."

"I don't understand."

"Unless provoked, his behavior is completely aligned with what's deemed socially acceptable."

"And when he is provoked?"

"When Sergei is provoked, people die, Angelina. Which is why, if you find him zoned out again, as you put it, you should stay back."

I stare at him, finding it hard to believe the person he's describing is the man who so tenderly brushed my cheek demanding to know who hurt me. "But he didn't do anything to me. He just . . . we just talked, and he returned to normal."

"Which is highly unexpected." Felix nods. "Still, you shouldn't do that again."

"Okay."

"One other thing. If you find him asleep, you will not, under any circumstances, approach him. You will turn around and leave the room immediately."

What a strange request. "Why?"

"Doesn't matter. Just do as I say."

"All right," I nod and heap more mashed potatoes onto my plate.

There is no way I'm buying this shit. He's exaggerating, probably trying to scare me into spilling the beans. Yes, Sergei acted strange last night and has a reputation as a slightly unstable guy, but no one is normal in our world.

I hear the front door open and turn to see the object of my thoughts come inside, holding a helmet under his arm.

"I thought you went shopping," Felix shouts from next to the sink. "Where are the clothes you brought?"

"Arriving by cab. I told the guy to bring the bags to the door."

Sergei throws the helmet on the sofa, takes off his jacket, and walks into the kitchen. As he passes my chair, he reaches with his hand and lightly brushes his palm down my arm, igniting goose bumps where our skin touches. And it's not a bad type of goose bumps.

"What's for lunch? I'm starving." He sits down in the chair next to mine and looks into the pot in the middle of the table. "Meatballs again? Jesus. I'm signing you up for a cooking course next week."

"If you have complaints about my cooking, feel free to start preparing the food yourself."

Sergei sighs, and starts piling the food onto a plate. When he's done, he looks down at his meal, curses, and digs in. He's obviously not pleased with what Felix prepared, but I don't see him going into a murderous rage or whatever. As I suspected, Felix was exaggerating.

Sergei's dog comes in from the living room, stops beside him, and starts nudging him in his ribs with its muzzle.

"Damn it, Mimi! I'm trying to eat." He moves the dog's head with his hand, but he does it with visible affection.

"Which breed is she?" I ask. I don't think I have ever seen a dog that big.

"Cane corso," he says between two bites. "I'm going to walk her after lunch. Want to come with us?"

Not a bad idea. I need to check out the area if I do manage to slip out at some point. "Sure."

We've just finished with the lunch when the doorbell rings.

"It's your stuff," he says to me and turns to Felix. "Can you get that?"

"Nope."

Sergei grumbles something in Russian and stands up. "Albert had a fight with his girlfriend yesterday, so he's cranky."

"Albert?"

"That would be me," Felix calls over his shoulder. "Sergei's take on a Batman joke. He thinks he's witty."

I raise my eyebrows. "Wasn't that Alfred? In the movie?"

"Yes, but he says that Alfred sounds aristocratic and I'm not sophisticated enough for it. So he changed it to Albert."

"Oh, well . . . that makes sense, I guess." I shake my head in confusion. Those two have a really weird relationship. I turn to see Sergei taking a bunch of bags from the porch and carrying them toward the stairs. There are at least twenty of them.

"What's that?" I ask.

"Probably the stuff he bought for you. Looks like he got slightly carried away."

I slowly turn and stare at Felix slash Albert. "How long does he intend to keep me here?"

"You'll have to discuss that with Sergei, I'm afraid."

I get up from the table, carry the plate to the sink, and then rush upstairs to do just that. Only I see a bunch of bags strewn all over the bed and Sergei gone. I'm wondering if I should check the other room I noticed on this floor when I hear the sound of running water coming from the bathroom on my right.

I head to the door and knock on it twice. "Sergei?"

He doesn't answer, so I try the handle and find the door unlocked. Without really thinking about what I'm doing, I open the door. And gape.

Sergei is standing in the shower while rivulets of water flow down his naked body. He is turned with his back to me, his head tilted up toward the spray. I follow the water trail with my eyes, from his wide shoulders, down his inked muscled back and then stop. Holy fuck! He has the most magnificent ass I've ever seen on a man. I should move away, close the door, and pretend I didn't see him. Instead, I keep staring.

"You are blushing, Miss Sandoval."

I gulp and look up to meet Sergei's blue eyes regarding me over his shoulder. As I stare, he slides the shower stall door to the side, steps out, and reaches me in a few big strides. I find it hard to keep my gaze focused on his face instead of letting my eyes wander downward, but somehow, I prevail.

"How long do you plan on keeping me a prisoner?" I ask, trying to pretend that I'm unperturbed by the fact he's standing in front of me completely naked. It's quite a feat. I'll add it to my resumé under "Other Accomplishments".

"Until you start talking," he says and places his hands on the door, caging me in against it. "You already know that."

"You can't just keep me here. I have a life."

"Tell me what I need to know, and you are free to go."

My concentration slips and my eyes slide down his front, and when I reach his crotch, my eyebrows hit my hairline. His cock is in absolute proportion with his body. Huge. I quickly snap my head back up.

"I told you everything I can," I say but it sounds more like a squeal.

"Then I hope you like it here, lisichka." Sergei smirks, and turns to grab a stack of clothes from next to the sink, giving me another view of his rock-hard, naked ass.

Finally, common sense kicks in and I spin around and head toward the bed, pretending to be engrossed in going over everything in the bags.

"I'm going to walk Mimi," Sergei says a few minutes later when he exits the bathroom. Clothed this time. Thank God. Or . . . Shame. "Are you coming?"

"Sure."

Sergei

I look down at Angelina, who is walking at my side, and barely manage to stifle a laugh. She's been feigning disinterest, but she's been inspecting the neighborhood while we've been strolling. The little fox is planning her escape route. It's hilarious.

Ahead of us, Mimi barks and runs toward old Maggie's garden, probably planning on digging out more of her flowers. She's been fixated on those flowers since last year.

"Mimi, *idi syuda!*"

Mimi looks at the flowers with regret, then canters toward us. She almost reaches us when she notices a couple walking a rottweiler down the street and instantly snaps to alert. I hurry toward her to make sure she won't attack what she may consider a threat, and at the same time, Angelina turns and starts running away. I laugh. It didn't take her long.

I stop next to Mimi, take her by the collar and watch Angelina for a few seconds. She's trying her best, but she's slow. Probably still weak from lack of nutrition. I point with my hand toward Angelina, giving Mimi the command for "protect", and cross my arms over my chest.

Mimi runs toward Angelina at mad speed and, halfway there, starts making a wide circle, to intercept her. Angelina changes her course, veering right, but Mimi keeps running a few meters in front of her, having a great time. My little fox realizes she's not going anywhere and suddenly stops, turns to face me with her hands squeezed tightly into small fists, and glares at me.

"She's herding me like cattle," she grumbles when I approach.

"She's guarding you."

"Like I'm a cow."

"Yup." I bend and grab her around the waist, then put her over my shoulder. "Today's prison break episode ends here."

"Put me down."

"Nope." I lightly tap her ass with my palm, then decide to leave it there. She might be skinny, but her ass is nice and perky.

"That's called sexual harassment," Angelina snaps. "Remove your paw from my butt."

"And what would you call sneaking into the bathroom while I was having a shower?"

"I did not sneak in. I just wanted to talk."

"You were ogling me. I'm just reciprocating in kind." I tap her sweet ass again and stroll casually across the park toward my house, waving to a mother who turns her children away from the scene.

"The moment I'm out of your clutches, I'm reporting you to the police."

"What for?"

"Kidnapping. Holding me hostage in your house. And sexual harassment."

"I'm sure the police would be thrilled to chat with Manuel Sandoval's daughter." I squeeze her butt cheek lightly, eliciting the most adorable, shocked gasp.

Angelina swats me on my back with her palm, and I laugh. She was a bit spooked the first day, but she doesn't seem to be scared of me anymore. People are always wary of me, so this is rather unexpected. It feels good.

"I have to go to a meeting tonight," I say, ignoring her protests. "Please hold any further escape attempts until I'm back. Albert is too old for chasing after you. He could have a heart attack, and who would cook for me then?"

"I'll take your request under consideration."

"Thank you."

"Can I get a laptop or something?"

"Nice try." I laugh. "No laptop. But you can ask Albert for a round of poker. Word of advice, though—he cheats."

"Cheats? He's seventy."

"Exactly. He cheats very well."

She arches her neck and looks up at me. "How much do you pay him?"

"I don't. I've been trying to get rid of him for years."

"I'm not sure I'm following."

I sigh and put her down on the porch. "Albert and I go way back. We worked together for a long time."

"Before you joined the Bratva?"

"Yes."

"And what did you two do together?"

"Sorry. Can't tell you that."

"Why? Was it something confidential?"

I look down at her, finding those dark eyes of hers watching me with a question in them. She was born into this life, so she's probably seen her share of nasty shit, but her eyes seem so innocent.

"Yes," I say and trace one of her perfect dark eyebrows with a finger. "And because you don't want to know. Trust me on that."

"How can it be worse than working for the Bratva?"

"It can." I place my free hand on the banister next to hers and bend until our faces are at the same level. Angelina's eyes widen, but she doesn't move away. We're so close I can feel her breath fanning my face as her breathing picks up. Slowly, I move my finger over her cheek and along her neck, then pause when I reach the spot where her pulse beats. It's strong. Faster than normal. "No more running away today," I whisper.

"Okay." She nods, without removing her eyes from mine.

I move my palm down her slender arm, lowering it over her hip, and press my hand to the side of her thigh, over the long thick scar I noticed while I was carrying her. "Who did this?"

Angelina's breathing picks up. "I fell from a tree."

I grind my teeth. She really should stop lying, it's definitely not her forte. I let my hand fall from her leg, and whistle for Mimi. "Come on. I have to change before I head out to that meeting."

Shevchenko is late, as usual. I take the mineral water the waiter brought over and observe the empty club. It's still early, people won't be arriving at Ural for at least a couple of hours. I prefer to conduct business in one of the warehouses, but Shevchenko insisted on a more public location this time. He probably got spooked when we last met. Coward. I lean back in the booth and call Felix.

"What's wrong?" he asks as soon as he answers the call.

"Nothing."

"You rarely call for *nothing*, Sergei."

"I was wondering what Angelina is doing."

"We had dinner, and I took her back to your room."

"Is Mimi in front of the door?"

"No, she's in the living room, where you left her."

"Go to the living room and put me on speakerphone."

"What am I? Your secretary?" he snaps.

"Stop grumbling and just do it."

"Fine." There are a few moments of silence. "It's on."

"Mimi," I say into the phone and hear her bark once. "Angelina. *Okhraniay!*"

"She went upstairs," Felix says. "Is that why you called?"

Nope. I called because even though I left my place barely an hour ago, I can't stop thinking about the little fox I left there. "Does she like the stuff I bought?"

"Why would that matter?"

"I'm just asking." I shrug.

"What the fuck do you think you are doing with this girl, Sergei? We don't know her agenda. A daughter of a Mexican drug lord doesn't end up as part of the cargo in a drug shipment on a regular basis."

"I'm not sure what you are hinting at."

"Oh? Let me enlighten you. Remember Dasha?"

My body goes stone-still. "Angelina is not a plant."

"You sure about that?"

"She's not an undercover agent, Felix. She is . . . too innocent for that."

"They all seem innocent. Until they try to slice your neck while you're sleeping. Consider your late wife before you even think about tangling yourself up with this girl."

"Angelina is not Dasha!" I bark.

"She speaks Russian, Sergei."

I sit up straighter. "What?"

"I checked her background. She studied languages and literature. She majored in English and Italian, but she also took courses in French and Russian. How convenient, yes?"

"It's a coincidence." I cut the call.

The waiter comes to ask if I want anything else, but I shake my head and focus on the entrance on the other side of the club. Could it be just a coincidence?

A group of men enter. Two guys in dark suits walk in front of a third one, partially hiding him from view, and both are scanning the surroundings. Shevchenko and his bodyguards. Looks like he's trying to make a statement by only bringing two men with him. The slimy bastard usually has at least five guys in tow, which isn't that strange given he would need several people to cover his enormous frame if shit did hit the fan. He's almost as large as Igor, Roman's cook, and that's not an easy accomplishment.

They see me and head toward the booth. It's only then do I notice a girl Shevchenko has with him. The bastard definitely likes them young. The girl can't be more than eighteen.

The bodyguards climb the two steps to the booth first and stand aside. Shevchenko follows, dragging the poor girl with him.

"Belov." He nods and takes the seat, pulling the girl to sit on his lap.

"You're late," I say, keeping my focus on the girl. I was wrong, she can't be more than sixteen, and based on the terrified look in her eyes, she is not there voluntarily.

"I had a meeting with O'Neil. He wanted to discuss a partnership."

"Oh?" I lean back and move my focus to Shevchenko but

61

keep watching the girl from the corner of my eye. "And what did Liam have to offer?"

"Same product. He said he's in the middle of negotiations with Diego Rivera, and should be able to deliver the quantities we need starting next month."

"We take seventy percent of Rivera's drugs. There is no way Liam can match either the quantities or the price."

"Well, he said that'll change soon." Shevchenko takes the bottle of whiskey the waiter brought over, fills his glass to the brim, and empties it in one tug. He pours another round, then places his meaty hand on the girl's naked thigh, squeezing it. The girl flinches and quickly presses her legs together, but Shevchenko opens them forcefully and starts moving his hand upward, under the hem of her short dress. The girl squeezes her eyes shut.

I look up at Shevchenko's bodyguards, then move my gaze to the bottle of liquor on the table. It should do.

"I am very excited to see how the Irish plan on accomplishing that." I lean forward, grab the bottle, and smash it against the edge of the table.

The girl screams while the bodyguards reach for their guns and turn toward the booth, but they're too late. I am already pressing the broken bottle to the side of Shevchenko's neck, right over his carotid artery.

"Put the guns on the table," I say without removing my eyes from Shevchenko's panicked face. Nothing happens.

I look up at his two men, who are standing on the other side of the booth with their guns pointed at me. I grab the hand of the one nearest to me and pull him across the table, shielding myself just before the other man fires. The guy I'm holding screams as the bullet hits his chest. I twist his hand which is still clutching the gun toward the shooter, and squeeze his fingers. The gun fires twice, catching the guy in the stomach both times. As he crumbles to the floor, whimpering, I use the broken bottle to slice the neck of the man I'm holding, then return my attention to Shevchenko. He is still seated, holding the girl to his chest like a sacrificial lamb. His eyes dart from me, over the bloody body sprawled on the table, to his man now lying unconscious on the floor.

"It distresses me when people point guns at me," I declare and motion toward the girl with my hand. "Come here, sweetheart."

Her eyes widen. She seems reluctant at first, probably because I have blood dripping from my hand, but then she gets off Shevchenko's lap and rushes to stand beside me.

"How old are you?" I ask, not removing my eyes from the horror-stricken bastard still sitting in the booth.

"Fifteen," comes a barely audible whisper.

Fifteen. Jesus Christ. She could be his granddaughter. "Go upstairs," I say through gritted teeth. "Ask for Pasha. He'll find someone to take you home."

I wait for her to leave, then approach the sick son of a bitch who is leaning back in his seat, as if that will help him. Tilting my head to the side, I size him up, then reach for the gun left on the table.

"I don't like child molesters." I raise the gun and shoot him in the center of his ugly mug.

After throwing the gun back on the table, I clean the blood from my hand with the corner of Shevchenko's jacket and turn around to find the waiter and a cleaning lady cowering in the opposite corner of the club, staring at me.

"Is Pasha here?" I ask.

The cleaning lady tries to take a step back, plastering her back to the wall. The waiter blinks and points up. I look up at the gallery suspended over the dance floor. Pavel is on the other side of the glass wall, holding a phone to his ear and looking in my direction. He's probably calling Roman to tattle on me. I hook my thumb over my shoulder toward the booth, then motion with my hand to signal that he should clean the mess. Pavel squeezes his temples with his free hand and shakes his head. I don't think he'll let me conduct meetings at Ural anymore.

My phone rings when I am halfway to my car. I fish it out and take the call without looking at the screen. I don't have to . . . I have a special tone programmed for my brother.

"Yes?"

"I'm going to fucking kill you!" Roman roars, and I quickly pull the phone away from my ear. The yelling continues for a minute or so, the usual warm family banter. All hearts and rainbows. " . . . chop you into small pieces, and then feed them to that beast of yours."

"Mimi doesn't eat raw meat." I put the phone back to my ear and light a cigarette. "It's bad for the digestive tract."

"You have a week to find me a new buyer. A week. You got that?"

"I already talked with the Camorra last week. They'll take twice the quantity we sold to Ukrainians. And, I have a meeting with some gangs in the suburbs this weekend. We're good."

"Damn it, Sergei." He sighs.

"Shevchenko said something interesting before I dispatched him. It was about the Irish."

"What?"

"They're in negotiations with Diego Rivera. Sounds like they plan on intruding on our turf."

"Oh, I'd love to see them try," he snarls. "No more killing off our buyers, Sergei. You hear me?"

"I'll try my best."

"He'll try his best. Wonderful," Roman mumbles into the phone and hangs up on me.

As soon as I park my car in the garage, I take a detour to Felix's place to take a shower and change. I tried not to get any blood on my shirt, but some ended up on my sleeve anyway. I don't want Angelina to see it or be afraid of me. Also, allowing her to see me covered in blood would require explaining.

When I'm done, I head into the house. There's no one downstairs, so I run upstairs and into my bedroom, where Angelina is curled on the recliner, holding a book in her hands. For a moment, I think she's reading one of my detective novels—I have tons—but I stop in my tracks when I notice the cover. She's holding *Anna Karenina*, Russian edition. Was Felix right about her?

She looks up from the book and meets my gaze. "How was the meeting?"

"Fine." I lean on the doorframe and nod toward the book she's holding. "You speak Russian?"

"Not exactly. I know some basics." She shrugs. "I took a Russian course my freshman year but eventually decided to focus on English and Italian."

"How much do you understand?"

"Well, I could probably ask for directions in Russian, and

I remember the names of some fruits and vegetables. I know a lot of curse words, though." She snorts, stands up from the chair, and walks toward the bookshelf to put the book back. "I loved the movie and wanted to try reading. I got stuck on the second sentence because *someone* wouldn't let me use the laptop to check the translations."

I leave my spot at the doorway, walk across the room until I am standing right behind her, and place my hands on the shelf on either side of her. Angelina sucks in a breath and turns around to face me.

"Are you lying to me again, Angelina?" I bend my head to look her directly in the eyes.

"About what?"

"Are you a spy, lisichka?"

She stares at me, then nods, her face a picture of seriousness. "Yeah. You totally busted me."

I narrow my eyes.

"I went through rigorous martial arts training as well, so you should watch your back when I'm around."

I look her over and burst out laughing. After her starvation, she's rail-thin and wouldn't be able to take on a squirrel. And even if she has lost some of her muscle mass, she doesn't hold herself like a martial artist.

When my laughing subsides, I study her. She's smiling, and I can't remember the last time someone teased me. "Tell me something in Russian."

"Now?" Her eyebrow curls upward. "What do you want me to say?"

"The first thing that comes to mind."

"*Sabaka Bobik,*" she blurts out.

I cringe. Her pronunciation is atrocious. "*Sabaka Bobik?* Where in the hell did you unearth that?"

"It's a cartoon character."

I cock my head and regard her as she chuckles. There is something about her . . . something that makes my demons sleep. I don't remember the last time I felt so calm in some-one's presence. Moving my right hand to the back of her neck, I bury my fingers into her hair. Her eyes widen, but she doesn't flinch as I expect her to, only watches me. There is no way she's a spy. Her face is like an open book, and, as I have al-ready concluded, she can't lie worth a damn.

That still leaves the question of what she was doing on that truck. I wonder about it for probably the thousandth time as I bend my head until my mouth is right next to her ear. "I will find out what you're hiding, eventually."

Angelina

I stand utterly still, trying to ignore the compulsion to lean in and inhale Sergei's scent. He is wearing that cologne again, the one that reminds me of how it felt to be pressed to his solid chest, with those strong arms holding me close. I am not an overly affectionate person, but I imagine my face snuggled into the crook of his neck while his hand slides up and down my back. Like he did that first night.

Sergei straightens, the tip of his nose brushing my cheek in the process, and my breath catches. My eyes follow him as he walks out of the room, and I still feel the goose bumps on the sensitive skin at the back of my neck where his hand has just been. This man is highly dangerous. I'll have to focus all my energy on getting out of here as soon as possible. This conclusion, however, has nothing to do with his reputation, and everything to do with the fact I don't like the way my body, as well as my brain, react to him. Being attracted to a person who keeps me prisoner is not normal.

A sound of loud barking outside reaches me, and I walk toward the window and look down at the patio in front of the house. Sergei is standing at the edge of the driveway, holding a stick while Mimi runs around him in excitement. He launches the stick toward the other end of the patio and Mimi dashes after it. For a dog that size, she is rather fast. I move my gaze back to Sergei, wondering why he insists on holding me here.

Does he really believe I'm a spy? If so, wouldn't it be more reasonable to have me gone? It doesn't make sense.

It's rather hard to connect the ruthless, crazy persona my father's men described, with the guy who is currently rolling on the grass with his dog, and laughing. A killing machine— that's how they labelled him. Felix also said a similar thing, so there must be some truth in all that, but still . . .

Placing my palm on the window in front of me, I watch the man who's been the center of my thoughts since the first moment I saw him.

Chapter
six

 Sergei

I PRETEND I'M ENGROSSED IN MY BREAKFAST WHILE
secretly watching Angelina on the opposite side of the
table. She's holding a spoon frozen halfway to her mouth,
and stares at Mimi who's nudging Angelina's side with her
snout.

"Relax. She won't bite you," I say.

"Are you sure?"

"She only bites people when I tell her to. And you're too
bony for her taste, anyway."

"Well, that's a relief, I guess."

"She wants you to pet her." I nod toward the dog. "If you
don't, she is going to pester you all day."

"She doesn't exactly look like a cuddly type."

Because she isn't. Mimi doesn't like new people. Or people in general, to be more exact.

Angelina reaches out to scratch the top of Mimi's head,
and Mimi licks her palm. The way my dog acts around her is
unexpected. She started following Angelina around the house

and always keeps her in sight, even without my commands. When Angelina sleeps, Mimi makes sure her head is precisely positioned where she can watch Angelina with one eye, while keeping the other on the door. It's the norm for protective dogs to place themselves between the person they're guarding and the source of a possible threat.

Maybe she's picking up the protective vibes from me. The image of Angelina curled up on the floor of that truck comes to mind, and I close my eyes, squeezing my fork. I will never forget the look in her eyes, like I was some kind of savior instead of a man whose main purpose was to end lives. It's been years since I felt the compulsion to protect anyone, except myself, and even that's rare. Most of the time, especially my last few years in the service, I didn't actually give a damn if I lived or not. But where Angelina is concerned, I have this inexplicable need to grab her and always keep her next to me, so no one can hurt her ever again.

"I played a round of poker with Felix the other night," she says. "You were right. He cheats."

"I told you." I snort. "What did you lose?"

"I have to prepare dinner."

"You were lucky. The last time I played with him, I lost my car."

"Seriously?"

"Yup. Then, I had to buy it back from him. He charged me twice the actual price. Asshole."

"Why didn't you just buy a new one?" She widens her eyes at me.

"I like that car. And I didn't want to deal with going to a car dealership."

"The dynamics between you two are really strange," she says.

"Yeah, you could say that. I often wonder how come I haven't strangled him yet. He nags me all the time, can't cook worth shit, and leaves his stuff all over my place." I shrug. "He did save my life a couple of times while we worked together, but he's losing those points rapidly."

"A couple of times? What were you two working on when he saved your life more than once?"

Oh, we are so not going there. I stand up from the table and whistle for Mimi. "Want to stretch your legs? I have to walk Mimi before I go to work."

She watches me for a couple of moments, then nods. "Okay."

"But no running away this time, Angelina."

She just smiles.

I throw the stick for Mimi to chase and turn around to find Angelina sprawled on the grass behind me, eyes shut and her face tilted to the sky.

"I feel like I've run a mile," she says.

"Tired?"

"A bit. My legs are shaking."

"Starving oneself can do that to a person." I sit down on the grass next to her, lean back on my elbows and look at the setting sun on the horizon. "You still don't want to tell me why you did it?"

"Nope."

"Then I guess you'll be staying with us."

"Not really. I need a few days to gather more strength, then I'll try running away again."

"Thanks for the heads up." I laugh.

She tilts her head to the side and looks at me with hooded eyes "Or you could just let me go?"

"Not happening. Sorry."

"Why?"

"I'm rather amused with having you here. Especially your fruitless escape attempts." I meet her gaze, reaching out with my hand to grab behind her neck, and lean to whisper in her ear, "And I haven't been amused for a very long time."

Angelina's already big, dark eyes grow impossibly round, and I wonder what she'd do if she knew the kind of thoughts running through my mind at this moment. Her. Naked. Pressed under my body as I pound into her with all my might.

I move my gaze from her eyes to the side of her chin. There is no yellowish tint there anymore. The bruise has disappeared, leaving soft healed skin. It doesn't matter, because I still remember how it looked. Someone had hit her before she came to me, and for it to leave the bruise that size, it had to be a very strong punch. Undoubtedly, it was a male who'd hit her. The familiar feeling of burning starts forming at the pit of my stomach, then spreads to my chest. My vision dims. Mimi starts barking somewhere behind me but the sound seems muted.

"Sergei."

It feels like I'm in a tunnel, isolated from the rest of the world. My vision dims even more. I can see Angelina's face in front of mine, she's saying something and the look in her eyes seems worried. I blink, hoping to clear my head. It works sometimes. Not now.

"Sergei!"

I feel small hands grab at my face, squeezing lightly. My hand is still at the back of Angelina's neck. I move it until I feel her pulse under my fingers, then press on it, focusing on the rhythm of her heartbeat.

"Are you okay? Sergei!"

My vision clears a little and Angelina's face comes back into focus. The feeling of isolation dissipates.

"Yes." I say, "Why wouldn't I be?"

Angelina tilts her head and looks at me with concern.

"You had that empty look in your eyes. And you weren't answering when I called your name."

"I was just deep in thought." I say and let go of her neck. "We should go back."

"Sure?"

"Yeah." I stand up and head in the direction of the house. For a dozen or so feet Angelina matches my quick pace, but then slows down to a sluggish walk. I stop to wait for her and when she catches up, she's breathing hard, so I wrap my arm around her waist and lift her in my arms.

"That's not necessary," she says, but doesn't make a move to get free. I ignore her comment, whistle for Mimi, and head down the path.

"Tell me, do all your hostages get the same treatment?" she asks a moment later.

"Me carrying them around when they're tired?"

"Yup." She nods.

"You're my first. I'm still going through a learning curve." I look down at her. "But you seem to be a pro in the hostage business."

Her brows shoot up. "How so?"

"I saw you smuggling the steak knife into the bedroom after lunch yesterday," I say and feel her tense up in my arms. "I also found the cleaver you keep under the mattress. Albert is particular with his favorite kitchen gadget shit. He'll go ballistic if he sees the cleaver gone. Can you swap it with the santoku knife? He never uses that one."

"How . . ." She stares at me. "Why . . ."

"Why didn't I take them away?" I smile. "Why would I? You haven't tried anything with them so far. And I think it's cute."

"Me keeping a meat cleaver under the mattress is . . . cute?"

"Very."

"You're weird."

"I'm not the one keeping a kitchen utensil in bed."

"It's a weapon!"

I imagine Angelina trying to attack someone with that thing and try to stifle a laugh, but fail. She would probably need to use both hands to lift it. Apparently, I may have offended her, because she juts her chin and snorts at me.

I enjoy the way Angelina feels in my arms. Having her this close ensures she's safe from anyone who might want to do her harm. When she tells me who hurt her, and she will eventually, I'll have such a great time killing them. I won't use a gun. That's too quick. A knife won't do, either. Hmm. Waterboarding? Maybe, if I can find a good place to do it. Strangulation? Yes, that sounds nice. As would cutting off their extremities. I'd need a chainsaw, and damn, that shit is loud. I'll consider it some more.

"What are you thinking about?" Angelina asks.

"Nothing in particular. Why?"

"Because you have a self-satisfied grin plastered all over the face."

"Oh, just planning some extracurricular activities, that's all."

CHAPTER
seven

 Sergei

I PARK MY BIKE AT THE END OF A LONG LINE OF HARLEY
Davidsons, remove my helmet, and lean on the handles,
inspecting the surroundings. Based on the sounds of
laughter and yelling coming from the bar in front of me, the
members of the Black Wings MC are having a great time. I
told Roman that doing business with MCs is messy, but since
my brother is mister bullhead extraordinaire, he insisted I
meet with them.

There's a sound of an engine nearing, purring softer than a
motorcycle, and a few seconds later, a sleek black sedan parks
to my right. Looks like my babysitter has arrived. After the
fuckup with Shevchenko, Roman ordered one of the guys to
go with me to meetings to ensure I behave. It's Pavel's turn
today.

The driver's door opens and he steps out. I stare at him
for a few seconds, then burst out laughing. "Are you fucking
kidding me?"

"What's wrong?" Pavel asks and looks around himself with disgust.

"What's wrong?" I motion with my hand in his general direction. "You do not come to a motorcycle club in a fucking three-piece suit. They'll think we're the fucking authorities."

"Oh, and what should I have worn to this meeting?"

"Jeans, Pasha. You do know what those are, don't you?" I don't think I've ever seen Pavel in anything other than a suit.

"I don't have jeans." He looks down at his gold Rolex and nods toward the bar. "Let's get this over with."

He doesn't have jeans. I shake my head and dismount the bike. Pavel and I are the same age, but it feels like he's fifty. "You should have been a banker." I snort.

The moment we step inside, all heads turn in our direction. There are a couple of seconds of utter silence, then a roar of laughter fills the room.

"Wrong place, pal!" someone yells. "The bridge club is down the street."

Another round of laughter follows us as we walk toward the table where the MC president is sitting. A woman is kneeling between his legs, with her mouth wrapped about his cock.

"Drake." I nod as I take a seat across from him. "Roman said you want to discuss some kind of collaboration."

He shoos the girl, tucks away his dick, and sizes up Pavel, who takes a seat next to me. There are seven MC members sitting around the bar, and a bunch of scantily clad women all looking in our direction, snickering. Pavel ignores them, leans back in his chair, and crosses his arms in front of him.

"I'm not discussing shit with Miss Priss here." Drake nods at Pavel. "I thought you were a serious guy, Belov."

"Oh, don't let the suit trick you, Drake. I bet that Miss Priss here"—I laugh—"can beat up any of your guys."

"Sergei," Pavel says in grave voice.

"What? It's the truth."

"We came to talk. Not to play," he grumbles.

"Oh, the candy-ass doesn't want to play," Drake roars with laughter, then turns toward the room. "This fine gentleman here just announced that he can take any of you on," he yells, pointing his thumb at Pavel, and the room erupts in laughter.

Pavel shakes his head, lifts his hand, and squeezes his temples. "You act like a nine-year-old, Sergei."

"Will you tattle on me to Daddy Roman again?"

"You slaughtered our buyer in my club two hours before opening. He would have found out anyway."

"Well, looks like it will be me calling the pakhan this time." I smile and nod toward the center of the room where one of the bikers is standing with his hands on his hips.

"Hey, pretty boy!" the biker shouts.

Pavel ignores him and turns to the president. "Can we discuss what we came here to discuss? I have work to do."

"You let pussies in the Bratva, Belov?" Drake snaps, then leans over the table into Pavel's face. "We don't do business with fucking cowards. When you claim shit around here, you prove it!"

Pavel turns his head toward me to give me an exasperated look, then gets up and turns to the bald-headed biker standing in the middle of the room. The guy is in his midtwenties, a little over Pavel's six feet two, and around seventy pounds heavier. I grin, grab the bowl of peanuts from the table, and lean back in my chair. This will be fun.

Another round of hysterical laughter erupts through the

room when Pavel removes his watch and starts methodically unbuttoning his jacket. However, when he places it on the back of his chair and brushes out the cresses on the shoulders, the crowd goes crazy. They even start cheering.

Pavel walks toward the biker and stops two paces in front of him. They are quite a sight: the biker—in jeans, with tattoos, bald head, and a biker's cut over his inked chest. And Pavel—with slicked back hair, perfectly pressed white shirt, and black vest.

Drake laughs. "I hope your pakhan won't mind him ending up dead."

"Not at all." I throw a peanut into my mouth. "But he says that kind of shit is bad for business." I take another handful of peanuts, then shout. "Pasha! Try not to kill him. Daddy will be mad."

The biker picks that moment to swing his fist. His face is all confidence. He clearly thinks he'll get Pavel with one blow. Pavel ducks. The biker's confused look is priceless. Pavel punches him in the stomach, and the big man stumbles backward. I laugh out loud. The biker is still trying to get his bearings when Pavel executes a perfect spinning back kick. The heel of Pavel's twelve-hundred-dollar shoe strikes the side of the goon's head. The guy tumbles to the floor, unconscious.

The laughter dies, replaced by a few murmurs.

"Man, I love that move," I mumble with my mouth full and turn to Drake. "Can we discuss drug business now?"

The president stares at me with his lips pressed into a thin line. "You piece of shit."

"What?" I light a cigarette and take a big drag. "Pasha was into the underground fight scene when he was young. I told you he could take on any of your men."

The low rumble of voices ceases, and utter silence remains.

"You came to my place to make a fool of me, Belov?" he bites out. "Was that your plan?"

"No, Drake. My plan was to see how serious you are about doing business. And based on what just happened, you seem more interested in brawling than collaborating." I extinguish the cigarette and wrap my hand around a half-full glass of whiskey on the table. "It really pisses me off when people waste my time."

I throw the liquor onto his chest, ignite the Zippo I'm still holding, and throw it at him.

Drake roars, jumps up from the chair, and thrashes around while flames eat at his clothes and skin. I drop to the floor, roll toward the end of the bar on my right and crouch. The sound of yelling and women's screams fills the room. Two of the bikers run toward the president, carrying jackets, ready to extinguish the flames. The rest are already grabbing for their weapons. I pull the gun from the holster on my ankle, straighten, and shoot three of the bikers, then duck back down. When I stand up again, I dispose of two more.

The group of women are hiding under the table in the corner, screaming. There is no sign of Pavel. His watch and jacket are no longer at the table. I leave my cover, shoot the last two men trying to extinguish the flames, then walk across the room, shooting each of the fallen bikers in the center of their foreheads. Never presume someone is dead until he's sporting a hole in his head. That's my motto. It even rhymes.

When I leave the bar I find Pavel leaning on the hood of his black sedan, with his hands in his pockets.

"That was rude," I say and grab my helmet.

"What it was is your fuckup. So, you should have been the one to handle it."

"Nope. It was thinking ahead. They would have turned on us at some point. Drake was already reaching for his gun when I roasted him."

"I'm sure Roman will value your foresightedness," Pavel says while getting into his car.

"Of course, he will."

Based on the amount of death threats Roman sends my way when I call him an hour later, he doesn't. My brother is unbelievingly ungrateful.

CHAPTER eight

Angelina

I LEAVE MY ROOM, OR BETTER SAID, CELL. MIMI FOLLOWS me as I head downstairs to see if there's something to eat in the kitchen.

After six days in Sergei's house, and two more failed escape attempts, I conclude that I will have to wait until I'm outside to try again. With alarms and remote locks on every window and door, and Mimi following me around nonstop, I have deemed the place escape-proof. Felix must have guessed my line of thinking because he told me yesterday morning that I'm allowed to walk around the house by myself. Probably because Cerberus is constantly at my heels.

Sergei hasn't been around much. From what I gleaned when he was talking on the phone, the Bratva had some problems with the Italians, and he needed to fill in for men who were hurt in some warehouse fire. I couldn't grasp all of the details. Regardless, I kind of miss seeing him. Could I be developing Stockholm syndrome?

Downstairs, I turn toward the kitchen, with Mimi trotting

behind me, but a sound from the living room makes me stop and turn my head. All lights except the lamp near the front door are off, so it takes me a few seconds before I notice Sergei. He's standing by the sofa with his back turned to me, looking at something on the wall opposite him.

"Hey, jailer," I say and head toward him.

He doesn't reply, just keeps staring ahead and lifts his right arm. A second later I hear a thump. I follow his gaze, and it takes me a few moments to focus on a narrow wooden board with a horizontal white stripe. It's similar to the one mounted on the wall in the room where I'm sleeping. The light is dim, but I make out several knives lodged in the board in a perfectly straight line along the stripe. Sergei lifts his arm again, holding another small knife, and sends it flying. It hits the board right next to its predecessors, extending the formation.

My eyes widen. "Wow. That's . . . impressive."

"Thank you," Sergei says in a detached voice that makes me look up at him.

He is standing completely still. Too still. Just like he was the night he was worried about his friend who got shot. I can't see his eyes in the low light, but if I could, I'm fairly certain they would be unfocused like then, too.

"Sergei? Are you okay?"

"Yes."

He doesn't sound okay.

I should use this opportunity to bolt. Mimi followed me downstairs, but when she saw Sergei, she disappeared. Felix isn't here. And in Sergei's current state, it's possible he wouldn't follow me if I try to leave. It's now or never.

I take a step back, turn and head toward the door. He doesn't follow. Only ten or so steps separate me from possible freedom. I'm wearing pajamas and my feet are bare, but I can't risk going back upstairs for shoes. Six steps. Five. He's okay, he'll snap out of his funk on his own. Three steps. I need to think about myself. I won't have an opportunity like this again. One step. I stop in front of the door and throw a look over my shoulder. Sergei is still standing in the same spot. I grab the knob.

"Fuck," I mumble, turn on my heel and head back.

Carefully I reach out and place my hand on Sergei's forearm.

"Hey," I say and squeeze him lightly. "Can you look at me?"

Exhaling, he bends his head and looks down, but I still can't see his eyes that well.

"Um . . . can you put away those?" I nod toward his left hand where he's still holding two blades.

He opens his fingers and the knives fall to the floor. Good. What do I do now? He still seems zoned out.

"What do you think about my pajamas? I didn't peg you for a baby panda lover."

My idiotic question is what finally gets his attention. He lowers his gaze to scan down my body, then lifts his eyes back up. "They're awful."

"You bought them." I smirk.

"Store attendant picked them out. She has bad taste."

"I think they're nice."

"Believe me, they're not."

I expect him to smile after that declaration, but he just keeps standing there. I don't like how still he is. Lifting my hand, I place my fingertip at the bridge of his nose and slowly trace a line along it, feeling a few ridges under the skin. It's the only imperfection on his impossibly handsome face. "How many times did you break your nose?"

"Four."

"You like bar brawls?"

"No. It happened during my training."

"What kind of training?"

"I can't talk about it."

It's strange how he can keep the conversation going while not being fully present. At least, I'm pretty sure that's what's happening. It seems like he's here, but at the same time, he isn't.

I reach out and place my hand on his chest. "Thank you for buying clothes for me. Feeding me. Washing my hair." I let my palm slide upward until it reaches his face, which is still set in hard lines. "Thank you for saving my life, Sergei."

He shakes his head and looks into my eyes. "Varya bathed you. Roman's housekeeper. I didn't think it would be appropriate for me to see you naked," he says, his voice sounding almost normal. "I just carried you to the bathroom, and then out when she was done."

"That was considerate of you." I take his right hand in mine. "I'm hungry. How about we go make me a sandwich?"

"Sure." Sergei blinks once, but it's as if his eyelids are moving in slow-motion. Then, his shoulders lower ever-so-slightly.

He's back. I let out a breath and turn toward the kitchen but stop. Felix is standing at the front door, watching us. The light from the lamp on his left illuminates him, revealing an expression of utter confusion mixed with surprise. I feel Sergei's body go rigid behind me. It lasts only for a second. He then lunges toward Felix, wraps his right hand around the old man's neck, and presses him against the door. I gasp and stare at

Sergei in shock. Felix doesn't move a muscle, doesn't try to free himself. He remains utterly still with his back pressed to the door, and Sergei's huge hand wrapped around his neck, as if this has happened before.

I take a step forward, but then Felix slightly raises his hand, signaling me to stay back.

"Sergei?" I say quietly.

Nothing. He tilts his head to the side and stares at Felix as if he's deciding how to end him. A low whimper comes from my right. Without taking my eyes off Sergei, I take two steps to the side and grab Mimi by the collar so she won't interfere.

"Sergei?" I call again, louder this time, and sigh with relief when he turns his head.

Now that there is more light, I can see his eyes are still slightly unfocused. I was wrong before. He is not fully here. I steal a quick look at Felix. Our eyes meet, and he gives me a barely noticeable nod.

"Come on, big guy. You promised me a sandwich. I still need to put on at least ten pounds to look like a human being again." I smile a little and extend my hand toward Sergei. "I don't know where you keep the bread. Please?"

Slowly, Sergei unwraps his fingers from Felix's neck and turns around.

"You're missing way more than ten pounds," he says. Approaching me, he grabs my hand and drags me into the kitchen, with Mimi following us.

"Ham or cheese?" He opens the fridge and starts taking out the food, his voice and behavior completely normal.

"Both. And lots of ketchup."

"That's disgusting," he says and looks over at Felix, who is now standing by the dining table. "Do we have ketchup?"

"No clue." Felix shrugs, goes to the cupboard, and starts taking out plates as if nothing strange happened a minute ago. "Maybe in the pantry?"

"I'll have a look."

Sergei leaves the kitchen, and as soon as he's gone, I turn to Felix. "Are you okay?"

"Yup. Why?"

Why? Is he serious? "Because Sergei almost choked you."

"He wasn't choking me. If he wanted to kill me, he would have snapped my neck." He turns to look at me. "I think he was keeping me away from you."

"That makes no sense."

"Was he having an episode when you found him?"

"An episode? You mean was he zoned out?"

"Yes."

"I think so, yeah. He wasn't responsive at first, but then he snapped out of it."

"How much time passed?"

"I don't know. A few minutes. I asked him to put down the knives—he was throwing them at the wall when I came in—and then, I asked some nonsense about my pajamas. I talked some more, and he came back shortly after that."

Felix stares at me unblinking. "He let you take his knives?"

"Well, he dropped them on the floor."

Steps approach, and I look up to see Sergei coming with a can of tomato sauce.

"I only found this," he says, then turns to Felix. "We're running low on potatoes."

"I'll order a delivery from the store tomorrow," Felix says as he places the plates on the table. "Text me if you two need anything else. I'm off to bed."

I follow Felix with my gaze as he walks toward the front door, but before leaving, he throws a quick look over his shoulder in my direction. It's rather strange, that look. Serious and calculating, and so very different from his usual casual demeanor. And, I realize that I'm not the only one under this roof who's been hiding stuff.

Felix

The moment I'm out of the house, I take out my phone and call Roman Petrov. He answers on the first ring.

"What happened?"

"You need to talk to the Sandoval girl," I say.

"About what?"

"We need her to come clean on why she's here. If she's a spy who somehow ended up with us, we need to know. And, she needs to be sent as far away as possible from Sergei."

"And if she isn't?"

I glance at the house behind me. "If she isn't, you need to convince her to stay."

"Stay where?"

"Here. With Sergei. At least for some time."

"How the hell should I convince her to stay? Why would she want to stay with Sergei? Are they fucking?"

"No, I don't think so."

"What the hell is going on, Felix?"

I stop in front of the garage and look up at the dark sky. "Your brother is not doing good." I take a deep breath. "He's been losing it more often in the last few months, and is barely sleeping. It started getting worse a couple of weeks ago."

"And you're only telling me this now?"

"You've had enough on your plate."

"We had a deal, Felix. You should have told me the moment he started getting worse. I sent him into the field for God's sake!"

"I thought it might help!" I snap.

"It obviously didn't! Did he tell you he offed Shevchenko on Monday?"

"What? No."

"How bad is he now?"

"Up until last week, it was really bad. But it seems as if he's getting better since the Sandoval girl came."

"Explain."

"She stumbled upon him while he was in a middle of an episode. Twice."

"Jesus fuck. Did he hurt her?"

"Nope. Somehow, she managed to bring him back both times."

"How?"

"I have no idea. She said she talked about her pajamas."

"She talked about pajamas?"

"Yes."

Roman laughs. "Well, they must have been a hell of a set of pajamas."

"They were covered in pandas, Roman. Regardless, you need to talk to her. If she can help Sergei, we need to keep her here."

"Have you been spending time with Maxim recently?"

"No. Why?"

88

"Because he's usually the one with crazy ideas." There are a few seconds of silence before he continues, "Okay. I'll call Sergei tomorrow and tell him to bring his cartel princess over to the mansion. And she better not be a spy."

"What do you plan to do with her if she is?"

"Kill her on the spot, Felix."

Chapter

nine

── • ──══ Angelina ══── • ──

I ENTER THE LIVING ROOM AND HEAD TOWARD THE SOFA, planning on watching TV for a bit, when I notice a stack of throwing knives on the table. Would Sergei notice if I took one? He probably would, and anyway, I still have the cleaver and the steak knife. He hasn't confiscated them. I'm pretty sure he noticed me slipping the scissors into my pocket this morning, but he didn't say anything. It doesn't seem like Sergei thinks I pose any kind of threat.

I don't have a problem with using violence to defend myself, but there has been nothing here to defend myself from. Other than the fact that I'm not allowed to leave, I've been treated as a guest the entire time. I don't know why I keep piling up the weapons.

If the shipment had been intercepted by one of the rival Mexican cartels, and they found me on that truck, I would have been raped—probably multiple times—and then sold. A shudder runs down my spine just from thinking about it.

I take one of the knives and hold it in front of my face,

inspecting its sleek shape. It doesn't look like an ordinary knife. There's no standard handle, and it seems like the whole thing is made from a single piece of metal. Based on its appearance, I expected it to be lighter. I turn toward the wall-mounted wooden board, where a few knives are still lodged, and walk across the room to inspect it closer.

There are six knives stuck in the board along the white stripe. They are so evenly spaced, it's as if Sergei used a damn ruler to make sure of their precise placement. I look over my shoulder, trying to calculate the distance between the board and the spot by the sofa where I found him last evening. More than twenty feet. My gaze travels back to the perfectly aligned knives. How is that even possible? There was barely any light in the room. I take a few steps back and narrow my eyes at the white stripe.

"You're too close," a deep voice says from behind me. In the next breath, Sergei's arm wraps around my waist and tugs me backward.

"Wouldn't it be easier if I'm closer?" I ask while my heartbeat picks up when he presses my back to his body.

"No. You need more distance so you can throw it properly." The arm around my waist tightens slightly, and I close my eyes, enjoying the sensation of his fingers trailing down my arm until he reaches my hand and takes the knife. "You start here." He lifts his hand that's holding the knife and slowly demonstrates the throwing motion. "One fluid motion. And you just release it. Do not flick your wrist."

Sergei releases the knife and it lodges itself into the board, right next to the previous one.

"What are those used for anyway? Can you kill a man with this?"

"In theory, yes," he says, still behind me, and then takes another knife. "In reality, it's too much bother. You need to calculate the distance, so the knife finishes its rotation just before it hits the target."

He lifts his hand, swings and throws again. Another perfect hit.

"If you're outside, you also need to consider the wind. And, if the target moves, you'll probably get them with an edge instead of the tip. Even if you hit them, it won't be lethal in most cases. It's much easier to approach and stab them."

"Why do you do it then? Why practice if it's pointless?"

"It relaxes me." He dips his head, brushing the skin of my cheek with his own. "Do you want to try?"

"Yes," I whisper, but the fact is, I'm not interested in practicing knife throwing.

His arm vanishes from around my waist. "We can do it tomorrow if you want."

"Sure," I say, mourning the loss of his closeness.

"We should get going. Pakhan wants to talk with you."

I pivot on my heel and stare at Sergei, trying to control the panic rising in my stomach.

"Why would your boss want to talk with me?"

"No idea." He shrugs.

"Do I really have to go?"

"You can't ignore the Bratva's pakhan when he calls you for a meeting." The corner of his mouth tilts upward slightly. "Unless you're hiding something really bad."

"Of course not." I try to pretend indifference. "What should I wear?"

"That'll do." He nods toward my jeans and T-shirt. "But bring a hoodie, and no flip-flops."

"It's ninety degrees outside."

"You'll get cold on the bike."

I raise my eyebrows and laugh. "I am not getting on that thing."

"Why not?"

"I like my body in one piece, thank you very much. Can we go by car?"

Narrowing his eyes at me, he places a finger under my chin and tilts my head up. "I would never put you in any kind of danger." He brushes my chin with his thumb, and instead of pulling away, I have to fight the need to lean into him. "If you're afraid of riding the bike with me, we'll take the car. But, I'd like to take you for a ride on my bike."

I look into his eyes, light and clear, so different from the way they were last night. Where does his mind go when he zones out? It can't be a nice place.

"You promise you won't let me fall off that thing?"

"I promise." He brushes my lower lip with his thumb. "I'll wait for you outside."

I stare at the door he just went through, wondering why his closeness impacts me so much. Saying that Sergei is good-looking would be an understatement. But still, he's keeping me a prisoner in his home. I shouldn't be attracted to him. Just the opposite. Shaking my head, I rush upstairs to the bedroom to grab a pair of socks and sneakers, my hoodie from the recliner and head back downstairs.

I regard the huge red bike parked on the driveway in front of me and wrap my arms around myself. Nope. Not happening. I don't even like bicycles. The idea of a vehicle that runs on only two wheels has never sat well with me.

Sergei approaches the bike, throws one leg over it, kicks up the stand, and sits down. "Hop on."

It suits him. The bike. I wonder what he looks like when he goes to a meeting. Does he wear a suit? I find it hard to imagine him in dress pants and a jacket. Or wearing a tie.

"Cold feet?" He smiles at me, and a pleasant warmth washes over my body. The need to be close to him overrides my urge to hightail it.

"No," I say. Taking a deep breath, I close the distance between me and that thing, and climb up behind him.

"Here," he says and passes me a red helmet.

I look it over, then put it over my head. It makes me feel like a giant ant.

"Arms around my waist and hold on tight. We'll go slow. If you want me to stop, just squeeze twice, and I'll pull over right away. Okay?"

Leaning forward, I plaster myself to his back and wrap my arms around him, feeling his rock-hard abs under my palms. Sergei puts on his helmet and starts the bike, and as soon as the engine roars to life, I press myself into his back even more.

At first, I can't think about anything except keeping my arms locked in a tight grip around Sergei, but after some time, I find enough courage to open my eyes and look over his shoulder. It's not that bad. As he keeps driving, excitement surpasses my fear. I've never been into extreme sports because I had enough excitement at home with all the raid attempts and random shootings around the compound, but this . . . I could get used to this. But more than the thrill of the ride, I'm affected by Sergei's closeness. It feels good, being plastered to his huge body in this way, and without actually intending to, I find myself leaning into him even more. I wish I didn't have the helmet on, so I could press my cheek against his wide back.

I'm not sure how much time passes, surely not more than half an hour, when Sergei takes a side road that goes slightly uphill toward the estate visible through the iron fence. He stops at the gate, pulls off his helmet and nods to the guard. After we pass, he drives for a minute or so and stops in front of a huge, white mansion surrounded by finely trimmed grass.

Sergei helps me get down from the bike, and I need a few seconds to acclimate to the solid ground under my feet.

"All good?" he asks after he takes off my helmet.

"Better than expected," I say and grin.

"Does that mean you liked it?"

"Maybe."

Sergei reaches to take a strand of hair that fell out of my short ponytail and hooks it behind my ear. His palm comes to cup my cheek and he tilts my head up so he can look into my eyes. An excited shudder passes through my body and I find myself leaning forward, with my gaze fixed on his lips. I wonder how it would feel, having those hard lips pressed to mine. A security guard opens the front door, bringing me back to reality.

"Let's get this over with," I mumble and take a reluctant step back. Sergei's hand falls from my face.

"Sure." He nods and heads up the steps toward the mansion door.

We enter the mansion and cross the big foyer, then turn to the left. At the very end of the long hallway, Sergei knocks on the door at the end, and we step inside. I try my best to keep my expression neutral, and my body relaxed, while in reality, I'm a bundle of nerves ready to explode.

Roman Petrov, the Bratva's pakhan, sits casually behind the desk on the other side of the room and follows me with his eyes. He is wearing a tailored dress shirt, the same shade as his ink-black hair, with the sleeves rolled up to his elbows.

There's a barely visible smile on his face, and I don't need a *Pakhan for Dummies* manual to know that it's not a good sign.

"Sergei," he says without removing his eyes off me. "I would like to talk with our guest alone, please."

Sergei places his hand on my upper arm. "Are you okay with that?"

Hah, like I have a choice. "Sure." I smile.

Sergei nods, then turns to Roman and points a finger at him. "Don't scare her," he says and leaves, closing the door behind him.

Petrov watches me, and the wicked smile on his face grows a little wider.

"It's good to finally meet you, Miss Sandoval," he says. "Please, sit."

My legs feel like they're locked in cement as I take a few steps toward the chair opposite him and drop down onto it.

"You needed to speak with me, Mr. Petrov?" I ask.

"I need you to start talking."

I sigh and close my eyes for a second. No one in their

right mind would lie to the leader of the Russian mafia. "What do you want to know?"

"Let's start with what the fuck were you doing stuck in the Italians' drug shipment."

"It was the only way to get away from Diego Rivera," I say.

"What does Diego have to do with anything?"

"Two weeks ago, he came to our compound under the pretense of talking business with my father. They were partners for years, so it wasn't unusual, and nobody suspected anything, even though he arrived with more men than normal. My father took him to his office. We heard the gunshots soon after."

Petrov leans forward, surprise visible on his face. "Diego killed Manny? I thought it was the police that killed him."

"That's the story Diego told everyone."

"I'm sorry about your father. We weren't on the best of terms, but I respected him."

"Thank you."

"So, Diego decided to take over your father's business, I presume."

"Yes. And, he concluded it would be more easily accepted by my father's men and associates if I was married to him."

"Of course, he did. So, how did you end up on that truck?"

"Diego was sending one of the girls with the shipment as a gift," I say, "I took her place."

Petrov tilts his head to the side, then leans back. "Okay,

let's say I buy that story. Why did you lie when Sergei asked who you are and what happened?"

"You're partners with Diego. If you knew who I was, and that he was probably looking for me, you would have sent me back." I fix him with my gaze. "I would rather die than go back and marry the pig who killed my father."

"So, what was your plan?"

"There wasn't one. My main goal was to leave Mexico and get to the US. I have friends here who would have helped me. I planned on contacting one of my father's partners to help me get documents so I can access my accounts, and then be as far gone as possible."

"Which partner?"

"Liam O'Neil."

"I don't think asking Liam O'Neil for help is a good idea, Miss Sandoval."

"Why not?"

"Because, the information I have says that Liam and Diego started working together."

I curse inwardly. There goes my plan for getting the documents. What am I going to do now?

Petrov watches me through narrowed eyes, probably wondering what the hell he should do with me.

"I have a proposition for you," he says finally.

"What kind of proposition?"

"I need help with something. You help me, and I get you the documents and anything else you need, and make sure Diego never finds you."

"And if I decline?"

"I tie you up with a bow and send you back to Mexico."

"So, you're blackmailing me?"

"Yup. It's worked great for me in the past." He smiles. "I blackmailed my wife into marrying me. Twice."

Poor woman. He's probably keeping her tied up in a room somewhere in the house. Bastard.

"What do you need me to do?"

"Nothing special." He shrugs. "Just stay where you are for the next couple of months. Let's make it six months, that's my favorite blackmail period."

I stare at him. "Sorry, I'm not following."

"I need you to stay with Sergei and keep doing whatever you've been doing so far."

"I wasn't doing anything other than sleep, eat, and wander through the house."

"There." Petrov smiles. "That doesn't sound hard, does it? Think of it as an impromptu vacation."

"That's ridiculous. Why would you want me to stay there and do nothing?"

"Because, my brother seems to have an unexpectedly positive reaction to you being there."

"Your brother?"

"Sergei is my half brother."

I look him over. They don't look anything alike at first glance, but now he's mentioned it, I can see the similarity in the lines of his face. The sharp cheekbones, the jawline, the build.

"You want me to play therapy dog for Sergei?" I ask, incredulous.

"Yes!" He hits the table in front of him with this palm, laughing. "A therapy dog. I couldn't have put it better myself."

"That's . . . crazy."

"Felix doesn't think so. He says that you've managed to snap Sergei out of his episodes. Twice."

"I didn't do anything. I just babbled some nonsense. Anybody can do that."

"Do you know what happened the last time someone approached Sergei while he was in that state, Miss Sandoval? The man ended up in an ICU for a month." He gets up, takes the cane leaning against the desk, and comes to stand in front of me. "You help my brother, and I help you."

"Or I'm getting sent back to Diego?"

"With a bow." His lips widen in a wicked smile.

"It's not like I have a choice, is it?" I sigh. The fact that I don't find the idea of staying repulsive should be seriously concerning. Stockholm syndrome was right on the money. "Did something happen to Sergei? Why does he have those episodes?"

Petrov grinds his teeth, turns toward the set of drawers on his right, and takes out a thick yellow folder, which he throws on the desk in front of me.

I pull the folder toward me, open it, and start leafing through the stack of papers. There are dates on each corner, starting eleven years ago. The last one is four years old. At first, I don't understand what I am looking at. It seems like they're some kind of reports, but most of the text is blacked out, and only parts of sentences here and there can be read. One thing that's common on all the documents is the signature at the bottom. Felix Allen.

"What's all this?" I ask, trying to grasp the meaning. I see some locations listed, mostly Europe, but there are some in the US and Asia as well. "Almost everything is redacted."

"The reports on black ops missions usually are."

My head snaps up. "Sergei was black ops?"

"A side unit. An experimental project where they took in teenagers no one would miss, usually homeless, and trained them into becoming operatives for the government's missions."

I look down at the stack of documents, flip back to the first page, and look at the date. "How old is Sergei?"

"Twenty-nine."

I do a quick calculation. "This means he started working for them at eighteen."

Roman waves at the papers. "Those are from when they started sending him on the missions. They took Sergei in when he was fourteen."

I stare at Petrov. That's not possible.

"What did he do for the government, exactly?"

"Whatever they needed that they couldn't achieve using regular channels. But, mostly, it was termination of high-level targets," he says.

Chills rush down my spine. "You mean . . ."

"Sergei is a professional hitman, Miss Sandoval."

I gape at him for a few moments, then drop my eyes back to the folder in front of me. There are dozens of reports there. The man who's been teasing me, who carried me around because I was tired, who bought me nine different body washes because he didn't know which scent I would like . . . who saved my life . . . is a professional killer?

Petrov leans in, takes the folder from my hands, and puts it away in the drawer. "It's not my intention to scare you, but I need you to understand what you're dealing with. I don't believe Sergei will hurt you, especially after what Felix told me, but if something happens that makes you think he is losing it completely, you need to pull back immediately. Do you understand?"

"Yes."

"Do you? Really?" He narrows his eyes at me. "Don't take this the wrong way, but you don't look like someone who could deal with Sergei's shit."

"Oh?" I raise an eyebrow. "And how do I look, exactly?"

"Like a librarian. You're only missing the glasses."

"What a coincidence." I cross my arms over my chest. "I applied for a librarian position at Atlanta University two months ago. Still waiting for their answer, though."

"Are you shitting me?"

"Nope."

He sighs and squeezes his temples. "Perfect. I just hired a fucking librarian to watch over a trained killer."

"Looks that way."

"Well, it is what it is." He shakes his head. "There's a fundraising party next weekend, and Sergei will have to go in my place. You will be going with him."

"I don't do parties."

"You do now. There will be a lot of important people there, and I need Sergei to behave. He never loses it when on business, but I don't want to risk it."

"I don't even know how to walk in heels."

"Then wear flats." He pins me with his gaze, which clearly says the discussion is over. "If you have questions, talk to Felix."

"Do you plan on sharing our agreement with Sergei?"

102

"No. I'll tell him what you told me, and say we agreed for you to stay until the situation with Diego is resolved."

"Okay. But I have a favor to ask."

"I'm listening."

"My nana stayed at the compound in Mexico. Can you try to get some information on her? To see if . . ." I take a deep breath. "If she's alive? I'm afraid Diego might have killed her because she helped me escape."

"The name?"

"Guadalupe Perez."

"If she's alive, do you want us to try bringing her here?"

"Yes."

He nods and extends his hand. "You help my brother. I get you your papers, and your nana."

I stare at his hand for a moment, feeling like I'm making a deal with the devil, then take it. We shake hands and I start pulling away, but his fingers tighten on my hand in a viselike grip.

"If you go back on your word,"—he leans forward until his face is right in front of mine—"you better pray Diego Rivera finds you before I do, Miss Sandoval."

He releases my hand and nods toward the door. "Let's go find Sergei. I'll walk you out."

As we leave his office and head down the hallway, the big double doors on the far side fling open and a petite, dark-haired woman runs out, holding a pot in her hands. She sees us coming and rushes toward us on bare feet.

"Roman! Help!" she shouts as the door behind her opens again and a rotund, bearded man in a cook's apron bursts out. He yells something in Russian, throws a kitchen rag onto the floor, with frustration apparent on his face, then turns and stomps back into what I assume is the kitchen.

The woman reaches us, laughing all the way, and halts in front of Petrov. "You want some Bolognese sauce, kotik?" she chirps.

Kotik? I blink. It means kitten in Russian. Did she just call the Russian pakhan kitten?

"Give me that!" Petrov barks and takes the pot from her hands. "What have I told you about carrying heavy stuff and running around?"

"It's five pounds, max!" She reaches to grab the pot back, but Petrov lifts his arm, holding it out of her reach.

"Angelina, this is my wife," he says, and I stare at the woman in front of me who is currently jumping up and down, trying to reach the pot.

"Stop jumping, damn it," Petrov snaps, "You'll give my child a concussion."

"Thief!" She scrunches her nose, pokes him in the ribs, then turns to me and offers me her hand, smiling. "I'm Nina."

She doesn't seem like someone blackmailed into a marriage.

"Thanks for the clothes." That's the only thing that comes to mind to say.

"Any time." She winks at me and starts to say something more when the front door opens and an older man in a suit rushes in.

"Maxim? What happened?" Petrov asks.

"Giuseppe Agostini had a heart attack. He died thirty minutes ago."

"Fuck," Petrov curses and trusts the pot into the older

guy's hands. "Get Sergei. I want you two in my office in five minutes."

Sergei

I focus on the picture hanging on the opposite wall, and try to reign in the need to storm out of the room and look for Angelina. As soon as Roman heard the Cosa Nostra don had died, he ordered Maxim and me into his office to discuss our next steps as far as the Italians are concerned. But, it's been hard to follow the conversation with Angelina still not at my side.

Sitting in the chair beside me, Maxim says, "Agostini doesn't have sons. I think Luca Rossi is the most probable successor. If that happens, do you think he will honor the truce we made with the don?"

"I only met him twice. He's a wild card." Roman places his hand on the table and starts his agitating habit of drumming his fingers. "Rossi is more into arms dealing than drugs, but that could change if he becomes the don. He will have to go with what most of the Chicago Cosa Nostra Family wants."

"Do you plan on meeting with him?"

"Let's wait to see what will come out of this shitstorm first. We'll continue our business as usual, but Maxim, send someone to keep an eye on the Italians," Roman says and turns to me. "There's a fundraiser for homeless kids next weekend. I need you to go and leave a big fat check. I don't want the city authorities looking our way for the next month or so. Can you handle that, or should I send Kostya? Maxim and I are stuck handling transportation until Mikhail is back."

"Kostya will only end up banging some official's wife in the restroom. I'll go." I nod.

"Good. The event requires a plus one. Angelina will go with you."

"Roman, I'm not sure that's wise," Maxim throws in. "What if someone recognizes her?"

"Last I checked, the cartel members don't frequent our government's fundraiser parties," he says and turns to me. "You're taking your cartel princess with you. And make sure you behave." He points his finger at me. "No weapons are allowed there."

"Sure. Is that all?" I can't take this anymore. I need to go find Angelina or I'm going to lose my shit in front of my brother. I know that nothing will happen to her while she's in Roman's home because this house is better guarded than Fort Knox. The fact that my fear is completely irrational does nothing to lessen the pressure.

"Yes."

"I'm off then." It takes tremendous control for me not to run out of the damn office and down the hallway.

I find Angelina in the lounge, laid back in one of the big recliners, while Nina is sitting on the floor in front of her and sketching something on a piece of paper. Nina is jumpy around me, so instead of going in, I stay in the doorway and watch Angelina play with a strand of hair, wrapping it around her finger. I remember it was once long. She looks up, and when she notices me, a strange look crosses her face, but then it's gone the next instant.

"Ready to go back?" I ask.

"Sure." She stands up and turns to Nina. "Can I see?"

"Of course not. It's just a sketch. You'll get the finished thing when I'm done." Nina hides the paper behind her back and looks over at me. "Is Roman in the office?"

"Yes. And he's exceptionally cranky." I reach out, take Angelina's hand, and the pressure in my chest subsides.

"What did Roman want to talk about?" I ask the moment I park the bike in front of my house.

"He wanted me to come clean with what I'm doing here." She sighs. "It didn't seem like a wise thing to keep lying, so I spilled the beans. Told him that I ran away from Diego Rivera. And Petrov promised he won't send me back to him."

"What does Diego have to do with anything?"

"Other than killing my father? Well, he locked me up in my room and started preparing for our wedding."

I feel my body go stone-still. "Diego killed your dad?"

"Killed him, took over his business, and decided to marry me by force. Yes."

The image of Diego Rivera touching Angelina with his meaty hands fills my mind, and the familiar buzzing sound starts filling my ears. "Did he do anything?"

"No, he didn't do any . . . Sergei?"

Her hand grips my forearm, and it grounds me a little. My demons are somehow afraid of scaring her, so they withdraw when she is near.

"Sergei, look at me."

107

A touch of her warm palm brushes my neck, then my face.

"Please don't zone out on me. Sergei?"

I blink, and Angelina's face is in front of mine, her palms pressed to either side of my face and her big dark eyes staring into mine.

"Are you back?" she whispers.

"I'm back." Fuck. I close my eyes. "So, what now? Do you plan on leaving?"

I'm not letting her go even if she says yes.

"Your pakhan said it would be wise if I wait until we see how the situation with Diego plays out."

"Good. You're staying here."

"You're not sick of me usurping your room yet?" She smirks.

"Nope." I take her hand and lead her to the house. "Let's see what crap Albert has prepared for lunch."

CHAPTER
Ten

I LOOK UP FROM THE BOOK I'VE BEEN READING TO follow Sergei with my gaze as he takes a change of clothes from the closet and goes into the bathroom. The sound of water running reaches me a minute later. The other bedroom must not have a bathroom. I try to remember if I've ever seen him go in there and can't.

Placing the book on the nightstand, I get off the bed and head out of the room, walking around Mimi, who is sleeping in the middle of the carpet. The door on the other end of the hallway is unlocked, so I open it and look around the almost empty space. There is a dresser on one end, two mismatched chairs in the other corner, and a pile of boxes near the window. No bed. A military green sleeping bag is spread out on the floor, with a folded blanket and a pillow placed atop it.

I go back to Sergei's bedroom and lean against the bookcase, facing the bathroom door and waiting for him to emerge. The water shuts off, and the door opens. Wearing sweatpants and a T-shirt, Sergei exits while drying his hair with a towel.

"Where have you been sleeping since I've arrived?"

He stops midstep and looks at me. "In the other bedroom. Why?"

"There's no bed there. You've been sleeping on the floor this whole time?"

"It's a nice floor. I've slept in worse places." He shrugs like it's nothing.

"You can't sleep on the floor in your own house." I sigh. "Do you want me to look for a hotel?"

"You are not going to a hotel. You're staying right where you are."

"But . . ."

"No buts. You're staying put."

"Then, I'll sleep on the couch downstairs."

He takes a few steps until he's standing right in front of me, puts his finger on my chin, and tilts my head up. "You're not sleeping on the couch, Angelina. And don't worry, I don't sleep much."

"How much is that?"

"Three hours. Maybe four."

"No one can function on that little sleep."

"Well, I don't function that well anyway. As you've probably already noticed." He laughs, but I don't find it funny. He needs help. The finger on my chin starts moving along my jaw, then over my neck until his hand ends up at my nape.

"Roman ordered me to go to some damn fundraiser tomorrow," he says. "You're coming with me."

"He told me. Are we going on the bike?"

It's really hard to concentrate on the conversation because with each word Sergei's head bends slightly, his mouth coming closer and closer.

"I'm not sure that riding a bike in an evening dress is wise."

"I don't have any dresses here."

His head dips even lower, while his fingers lace into the hairs at the base of my neck, squeezing and coaxing me to tilt my head up.

"We will buy one tomorrow." His voice is deep, huskier than normal, and his lips brush mine as he speaks, but only for a fraction of a second.

"How will I pay you back? I don't have any money right now."

He watches me, then closes the distance between us as his lips crash against mine. It's like thunder and lightning. Hard, unexpected, deafening, and blinding. There's no time to think about what I'm doing, and I don't have the will to resist, so I don't. I grab at the fabric of his shirt and rise onto my tip-toes, trying to get closer. Sergei's hand squeezes the back of my neck, his other hand caressing the small of my back, pressing me tighter against his body while he attacks my mouth.

It's not enough. There was a pile of books on the floor somewhere. I couldn't decide what to read. I take a step to the left. Where's that fucking TBR pile when I need it, damn it? Why can't I be taller? Sergei's mouth leaves mine and proceeds to trail kisses along my jaw and neck. I suck in a breath and pull on his shirt even more as a tingling sensation starts building between my legs. I need him closer. My toes hit something solid. Yes! I step up onto the stack of hardbacks I piled on the floor and wrap my arms around Sergei's neck. My mouth finds his again. The hand at my back moves lower to squeeze my ass, then traces around my hip until it reaches the front of my jeans. He slides his palm lower and cups my pussy over the fabric, pressing the denim seam into my core.

"Sergei!" Felix shouts from somewhere in the house.

Not fucking now! I grip Sergei's hair, trying to keep his lips from leaving mine as I feel myself getting wetter and wetter. He starts brushing his palm between my legs, forward and back. And I think I'm going to ignite under his touch.

"Sergei!" Another round of yelling from downstairs. "Your brother is sending his regards with an extremely vivid description of cutting off your head and stuffing it into your anus if you don't answer your phone."

My eyes snap open and I stare at Sergei. He still has his hand between my legs. As I look into his eyes, he presses onto my frustrated pussy again, and a small moan leaves my lips.

"There." He smiles and lightly bites my lower lip. "Consider the dress reimbursed in full."

His hands vanish from my body, and he's gone the next moment, leaving me in the middle of the room, standing on an assortment of genuine leather-bound Dostoyevsky hardcovers, with my panties completely drenched.

The following morning, I find Felix fumbling with an electrical socket above the stove. He looks me over, then resumes what he's been doing.

"Is Sergei out?" I ask and sit at the dining table.

I haven't left the room since yesterday evening, trying to avoid Sergei until I manage to process the meaning of that kiss . . . or the entire encounter for that matter. Thinking about it didn't help much. I still can't decide if I should ignore it completely and pretend it never happened, or jump all over him the next time I see him. My brain says the former. My body wants the latter.

"He's walking Mimi," Felix calls over his shoulder. "I heard you're staying. Roman spoke to you yesterday?"

"Yes." I nod and reach for the carafe of juice on the table. "I think we should talk."

"About?"

"About those episodes Sergei has. I need to know what I'm dealing with."

Felix leaves the screwdriver on the counter, turns, and fixes me with his gaze. "You're dealing with the result of what happens when you take a nonviolent child and forcibly turn him into a cold-blooded killer." He places his hands on the counter, gripping its edge, and looks over at the window.

"Sergei was a normal kid. Loved. But then his mother died when he was only twelve, and he was sent to foster care and later to a group home. There were some brawls, small thefts, nothing that wasn't unexpected of a child in his situation. He ended up in a juvie after he and his friends tried to steal a car. That's where Kruger found him."

"Kruger?"

"The man in charge of the Project Z.E.R.O. unit. They took him in and put him into training. I was a handler there. From the moment I saw Sergei, I knew he wasn't a good candidate. He was not aggressive or violent, and didn't have the urge to hurt anyone or to destroy things like some of the other boys they took." He turns to look at me. "I tried to send him back, and failed. Kruger liked him too much. Sergei was impossibly agile, and he always got the best results during physical exams. He also spoke English and Russian perfectly, as well as Spanish. Kruger liked that very much. Fluency in several languages is very useful in our business."

"You helped make boys into killers?" I stare at him with disgust. "What kind of person does that?"

"A person who works for the government." He sighs and shakes his head. "I'm not proud of some of my choices, Angelina, but I've tried my best to correct my mistakes as much as possible."

He walks toward the bowl of fruit on the table, takes an apple, and starts rolling it in his hand, seemingly focused on a single blemish marring its otherwise perfect yellow skin.

"I first noticed signs that something wasn't right after Sergei came back from a mission in Colombia," he continues. "During field missions, his performance was impeccable. But when he would get back, he'd just sit down and stare in front of him for hours. Physically he was there. But mentally, he was away. One time, one of the guys from his unit stumbled upon him while Sergei was zoned out. I'm not sure what happened exactly, but I assume the guy tried poking Sergei with the knife we found next to his body later."

"What happened?"

"Sergei broke his neck," Felix says. "It got worse after that. He started getting violent every time someone approached him during one of his episodes. He also started having problems differentiating the field missions from everyday situations."

"How so?"

"Most of Z.E.R.O. unit's training consisted of extinguishing any trace of empathy or consciousness in the operatives, making them focus on completing the mission no matter what. Some missions, usually those that involved high-profile targets, resulted in significant collateral damage."

"What kind of collateral damage?" I ask as dread starts to build at the bottom of my stomach.

"If a certain person needed to be eliminated, and the only way to do so was to blow up half of the building, it was deemed acceptable. Those situations were rare, but they happened. Sergei performed the missions without fail, but then, his behavior would turn extreme when he was out of the field. One time, he saw a man mistreating a homeless woman and gutted him on the spot. He didn't feel he did anything wrong. In his mind, he neutralized the threat and that was it."

"Petrov said you managed to get him out, eventually."

"Yes, but it was too late. When Sergei started losing it more frequently, I pulled some strings to get us released. I contacted Roman soon after. He had no idea that he had a brother. Sergei knew about Roman, though. His mother told him that Lev Petrov was his father and that he had a half brother. But Sergei never wanted anything to do with Lev or Roman. I had to do it behind his back, and he almost strangled me when he found out."

"And why hasn't anyone tried to get him some help? Counseling? Anything?"

"Sergei is not just a trained killer, Angelina. He's a top-of-the-line government weapon. The best-case scenario would be Sergei ending up drugged and tied down in some institution." He looks up at me, squeezing the apple in his hand. "The worst would be the government neutralizing him the moment they got him. Sergei knows too much, but as long as he's a part of the Bratva, they won't touch him. Roman pays a lot of money under the table to make them look the other way."

"Has anyone tried to help him? Or does everyone just avert their eyes and wait for a miracle?" I throw my hands in the air with frustration. "He calmed and came back when I spoke to him. Maybe he just needs to know that someone is there for him, damn it."

"He would kill anyone who gets close to him when he's in that state, Angelina." Felix looks down at the floor. "I don't know why he reacts the way he does around you. I've been with him for fifteen years, and I don't dare approach him when he's out. You may have awoken some protective instinct in him. When he brought you here that night, he wouldn't let anyone get close. We barely managed to convince him to let the doctor check you out, and for Varya to bathe you."

"You think he can get better?"

"I have no idea." He shrugs. "But you need to keep one thing in mind. If I'm right, and Sergei for some reason thinks he needs to protect you, he won't be reasonable."

"What do you mean?"

"I mean, he will kill every person he feels may be of any kind of threat to you. Real or imagined."

CHAPTER
eleven

 Sergei

I TRACK ANGELINA WITH MY EYES AS SHE LEAVES THE changing room and brings a bundle of silk to place it on the counter in front of me.

"Gold?" I ask.

"Yup. Looks more glam. Have to compensate for the fact I'm going in flats."

"Not a heels girl?"

"Nope. Regina, my friend from college, once convinced me to wear her four-inch-high sandals when we went out. I almost broke my neck."

I smile and give the cashier my card, while Angelina fidgets next to me. She's been nervous the whole day, but pretending nothing has changed. I keep expecting her to mention last night's kiss, but nothing. She sure as hell was eager, but the kiss was so innocent, I don't think she has much experience. So, I've had to resist making any more moves on her so far today. But, as soon as we get back from that damn fundraiser tonight, we will be continuing where we left off.

"Marlene booked you an appointment for some beauty grooming thing," I say. "We're going there next."

"Grooming?"

"Haircut. Smearing goo on the face. Eyebrow plucking. That kind of crap."

Angelina snorts and shakes her head. I like the way she looks at me, I don't quite remember the last time someone other than Felix looked at me like I'm a regular guy. Not this fucked-up-in-the-head person everyone feels the need to walk on eggshells around.

"Lead the way to the grooming salon, then." She takes the bag with the dress. "Can't wait to be plucked and smeared in goo."

We leave the store, and, wanting to avoid the crowd, I take a shortcut to the parking lot and turn into a side alley. A delivery guy parks his motorbike some distance in front of us, takes a box from the back, and hurries in our direction. As he passes us, he trips over a cobblestone, stumbling into Angelina in the process.

It was an accident, I know that. He barely even touched her, but my brain completely discards that fact, and, as if on its own accord, my hand lashes forward and grabs him by his jaw. The box he was holding tumbles to the ground. The guy gasps, his eyes going wide. His hands scratch at my fingers, trying to free himself from my hold.

"Sergei . . ."

I hear my name being called, but it feels like it's coming from somewhere far away. I ignore it and bend my head until I'm face to face with the bastard who hurt my girl. He must die. I move my hand lower until my fingers are wrapped around his neck and start squeezing.

"Sergei . . ." A small hand lands over mine and brushes my fingers lightly. "Let him go."

No. He hurt her. I exhale through my nose and squeeze harder, enjoying the way the guy's eyes bulge as he fights for breath. I could have just snapped his neck, but that would have been too easy. I add a bit more pressure. The guy starts choking.

Angelina's hand vanishes from mine, and in my peripheral vision, I see her running to the box the guy dropped and pushing it toward me. I want to ask her what the fuck she's doing with that thing, but I can't make myself let go of the guy's throat. The need to just end the threat he represents is too strong, so I squeeze a bit more. Angelina pushes the box somewhere behind me and disappears from my sight. I put my other hand on the guy's neck, intending to break it, as something large lands on my back. I gasp for air. Arms wrap around my neck from behind, and legs around my waist, squeezing me.

"Sergei," Angelina whispers into my ear, her breath fanning at my skin. "Look at me. Please."

I take a deep breath. Then another one. Angelina squeezes her arms and legs tighter around me.

"Please, look at me, big guy."

The heat of her body seeps into my back, her breath brushes my ear, and then a kiss lands at the side of my neck. I am trying to focus on the guy I'm holding, but her closeness is distracting me.

"I can't hold myself like this for much longer, Sergei," she says as her hold around my neck loosens a bit.

I let go of the motherfucker, and grab her under her thighs, saving her from falling.

"How the fuck did you end up there?" I ask, keeping my eyes on the delivery guy kneeling on the ground in front of me, coughing.

"Climbed the box," she says next to my ear. "Then jumped on your back."

"Why?"

"Why not?" she chuckles.

I turn my head to the side, bumping into her nose with my cheek.

"Why not?" I repeat and laugh. "Well, I guess that's as good as any other reason."

"I'm going to be late for my goo appointment," she says and squeezes her legs around my waist. "Can we head to the beauty salon now?"

I look down at the guy, who is still panting. "Watch where you're going next time."

He nods quickly, staring up at me. I walk around him and head down the alley. "Are you getting down?" I ask as I walk.

"Nope. I kind of like it up here."

"Okay." I bend and scoop up the bag with her dress that I dropped earlier.

I take my phone and scroll through the news. I can't concentrate, so I throw the cell on the dash and glare at the entrance of the salon. Three and a half hours. What the fuck have they been doing to her for three and a half hours?

The girl who came to lead Angelina inside told me that it would take a while, and that I should go for a walk and come back later. Leaving was out of the question, of course, so I sat in the waiting room next to an older woman with pieces of aluminum foil sticking out of her hair and fidgeted with my phone. Soon afterward, another woman wobbled in from one of the rooms, walking on her heels with some pink foamy shit stuck between her toes. It looked painful. She came to sit on the other side of me, looked me over and started a conversation with the woman on my right. When the discussion switched from hair products to homemade constipation recipes, I decided I had enough and went to wait in the car. That was three hours ago.

What if Angelina changed her mind and decided to hightail it? Can't say I would blame her. Anyone in their right mind would run away from a lunatic, so maybe she decided she'd be safer away.

I've kept an eye on the entrance the whole time, but maybe they have a back exit. Shit. I leave the car and rush inside the salon just as Angelina emerges from the left-side hallway, and the panic that's been building dissipates.

"So? What do you think?" She juts her hip and raises her eyebrows.

I look her over. Other than her hair, which is a bit shorter and straighter, she looks the same to me. Even covered in mud she was beautiful, so I'm not sure what she is expecting me to say. I guess after enduring three and a half hours of torment, she needs confirmation of a job well done or something.

"I like the hair?"

Angelina sighs and shakes her head. "You are a lost cause."

"What did you want me to say?" I ask as I pay the salon assistant.

"How amazing I look?"

"You looked amazing before we came here. What have

you been doing in there for almost four hours? Watching Netflix?"

She tilts her head to the side and pouts. "You have an interesting way of giving compliments."

"I was just making an observation." I shrug, take her hand, and head to the car. "We should hurry. Those fancy motherfuckers don't like it when people are late to their events."

"And what's the purpose of this event?"

"Roman is bribing the city officials."

"Publicly?" She gapes at me.

"He gives money under the table as well, but he likes to make donations publicly, as well. He's snobbish that way."

"Why doesn't he go himself?"

"A payback, probably. He said he doesn't have time for it, but I think he's still angry with me for . . . let's say, breaking our connections with Ukrainians."

"What did you do?"

I glance down at her, wondering if I should tell her the truth. She's staring up at me with those chocolate eyes, waiting for my answer, and I can't make myself tell her. Angelina is no shrinking violet. She must know how business in conducted in our world, but I don't want her to fear me.

"Just, terminated the contract," I say finally and open the car door for her.

CHAPTER
Twelve

 Angelina

I LOOK AROUND THE BIG HALL WITH WIDE EYES, admiring the gigantic crystal chandeliers and the gold decorations on the walls, then straighten my dress self-consciously. I feel completely out of place here. Turning to my side, I glance at Sergei, who is standing next to me, watching the crowd.

I usually see him in jeans and a T-shirt, but right now, he's wearing a gray dress shirt and a custom tailored black suit that fits him like a glove. He looks devastatingly handsome.

"Let's just leave the money and get lost," he mumbles.

We walk toward the table covered with a white silk table-cloth and flower arrangements. Two men in expensive suits stand next to it, talking with a group of laughing women in fancy gowns. When we approach, I decide to stay a few paces behind and watch Sergei as he shakes hands with the men. They exchange a few words, then Sergei takes out an enve-lope, which I assume contains a check, and places it on the table in front of a woman collecting the donations. The man on his left, a short bald guy in a suit that's a little too tight around the middle, smiles and taps Sergei on the shoulder. Sergei nods, bends his head, and whispers something in the man's ear, and the guy beams.

"What did you tell him?" I ask when Sergei comes back.

"The amount written on the check."

"Based on his grin, I assume it was a very nice one."

"One million."

My eyes widen. "Wow."

"Yup. Playing nice with the authorities tends to be expensive." He nods toward the exit. "Let's go. Politicians always give me the creeps. When we get home, we can take the bike and go for a ride."

As we walk across the hall my eyes land on a man talking with a woman in the corner. He seems vaguely familiar, but I can't place him. I shouldn't know anyone here. They're mostly high-level officials, not the people I would have ever come in contact with. I shake my head. Maybe he just reminds me of someone. We're at the door when it hits me, and I stop in my tracks.

"Shit," I mumble.

"What is it?"

"Was that Angelo Scardoni in the room?"

"Yes. Why?"

"He visited my father a few days before Diego came. It was something about business. I was at the compound, and he saw me in passing. What is he doing here?"

Sergei takes my forearm and turns me to face him. "Did he recognize you?"

"I don't think so. He was talking with someone."

He watches me for a few seconds, then takes the car keys

from his pocket and places them in my hand. "Wait for me in the car."

"Why?"

"I need to have a little chat with Scardoni."

Based on the murderous look in his eyes, I don't think he plans on just talking.

"There's no need. If he saw me, he would have probably said something."

"I'm not risking it."

"You're just going to talk with him?"

"Yes."

"Okay." I nod and watch him as he goes back into the hall, then head outside.

Inside the car, I spend twenty or so minutes setting up the phone Sergei gave me before we headed to the party. He just put it in my hand and said that he programmed his and Felix's numbers. It surprised the hell out of me. I guess he doesn't think I'm a flight risk anymore.

I'm replying to Regina's panicked email—the eleventh in a row—ensuring her that I'm okay, when the driver's door opens and Sergei gets inside.

"Scardoni didn't see you," he says and starts the car.

"Are you sure?"

"I am now." Sergei smiles.

As he reverses, I notice a male figure wobble through the service exit, holding his arm around his middle, and head to one of the parked cars. He takes a hold of the car door, then looks up in our direction.

"Jesus, Sergei," I snap. "You said you were just going to talk with him."

"We did talk. He said you looked familiar." He shrugs. "I

convinced him he was wrong. He's now absolutely positive that he never saw you."

"Is this your usual MO?"

He turns his head to look at me, reaches toward me with his hand and traces a line along my chin. "Nope. If he were anyone else, I would have just disposed of him. The only reason he's still breathing is because he's Mikhail's brother-in-law."

"Don't you think it's a bit extreme?"

Sergei pulls the car over in front of a closed car wash, then grabs me by the back of my neck, and leans into my face. "I will eliminate anyone who might pose even the slightest threat to you, Angelina. If I, even for a second, suspected that he recognized you, he would have been dead."

"Sergei . . ."

"No one. Threatens. Your. Safety," he bites out. "Got that, Angelina?"

I blink, then nod.

"Good," he says, squeezes my neck, and slams his mouth to mine.

I suck in a breath. He's wearing that cologne again, the one that messes with my head. Grabbing at his shoulders, I climb onto his lap and press my core to the bulge in his pants. The moment I feel his hard cock against my already tingling pussy, a shudder passes through my body.

Sergei

My cock is so hard that it feels like it's going to explode, and having Angelina rub against it with her pussy makes it a hundred times worse. I slide my hands down her body, gather the fabric of her dress in both hands, then push it up to her waist. Gripping the back of her neck with one hand, I slide the other between us, and press my fingers to her panties, finding them completely drenched.

"So fucking wet for me already." I move her panties to the side and thrust my finger inside her.

"We'll get arrested." Angelina gasps, then moans when I add another finger. Then, she starts rocking her hips, riding my hand.

"My greedy little fox . . ." I whisper into her ear and bite her earlobe. "Is my finger enough, or do you want more?"

"More." She breathes and then groans when I pinch her clit.

"I don't have a condom here, baby. But, I get tested regularly. I'm clean."

"I'm on birth control. I got the shot last month." Angelina assures me, then moans again.

I bury my face in her neck, inhaling her scent, and reach for the button on my pants just as my phone starts vibrating on the dashboard. Then ringing. It's Coolio's "Gangsta's Paradise" melody, the ringtone specifically for Roman's calls.

Fuck. I lift my head from Angelina's neck and reach for the phone, keeping my hand occupied with her pussy.

"Not now, Roman," I say and cut the call. It starts ringing again.

I push my fingers deeper inside Angelina and take the call.

"That's the first and the last time you hang up on me," Roman barks. "Got that?"

"What is it?" I put the phone between my shoulder and

my chin, and proceed massaging Angelina's clit with my thumb, while sliding the fingers of my other hand in and out.

"O'Neil just called," Roman says.

"Interesting." I pinch Angelina's clit lightly and smile when she whimpers. "What did the Irish want?"

"He wants to meet. Tonight. They have a deal with the Romanians for some weapons shipment that ended up being larger than expected, and wanted to see if we are interested in joining in on the deal."

Angelina's hands find the zipper of my dress pants. She realizes that I didn't wear any boxers tonight and she easily frees my cock. When she squeezes it, I barely manage not to come. I lean forward and lick the arch of her naked shoulder.

"He knows we take the guns from the Albanians," I say and slide my finger out of Angelina's pussy, switch the call to speakerphone, and throw the thing onto the passenger's seat. Taking a hold of her panties, I tear at the material and throw the black lace onto the back seat. Grabbing her under her ass, I lift her and position myself at her entrance. Angelina leans in, crushes her lips to mine and lowers herself slowly onto my cock, moaning as she takes all of me. Her panting is getting louder as she starts riding me, so I press the finger that was just moments ago buried two knuckles deep inside her pussy into her mouth. Her perfect lips close around it, and she starts sucking. My cock jumps inside her. I need to get off the fucking phone. Pronto.

I hear Roman saying something else, but I ignore his rambling. Removing my hand from Angelina's mouth, I put my finger over my lips in a hush signal. When she nods, I take her around her waist, lift her, then slam her down onto my cock. She screams a little, then rocks her hips, her hands tangling in my hair.

"Sergei!" Roman's yelling comes from the phone. I reposition Angelina slightly and then slam into her again, panting.

"What?" I bark and slam into her again, enjoying her little moans.

"Where the fuck are you?"

"In my car. With Angelina." I slide my hand between our bodies and pinch her clit, and she whimpers loudly.

There are a few seconds of silence, and then Roman's growly voice fills the car. "Are you having sex while you're on the phone with me?"

"Maybe." I smile, grab Angelina's nape, and crush my mouth to hers, all the while pounding into her.

"Jesus, Sergei," Roman snaps and hangs up.

Angelina's body starts shaking, her walls squeezing my cock. She's so alluring with her hair tangled and falling over her flustered face. I grab a fistful of the black strands and thrust inside her, hard. A slight sound, like a kitten purring, leaves her lips. Hearing it, combined with the way her tight pussy is gripping my cock when she comes, throws me over the edge. I slam into her like a madman until my seed explodes inside her.

She mumbles something incoherent, sighs, then sags onto me, burying her face in the crook of my neck.

"You okay, baby?" I ask.

"Yes," she whispers and nuzzles at my neck.

I smile, place a kiss on the top of her head and dial Roman.

"Done already?"

"Fuck you, Roman." I lean back and brush my palm down

Angelina's back. "Why would the Irish offer us an in for that shipment?"

"So, you also think that this stinks?"

We're not on good terms with the Irish. They don't come onto our turf, we don't tread on theirs. You could say we're putting up with each other's presence, but each would be very happy if the other ceased to exist. Having O'Neil call Roman only two weeks after he practically declared that they would try to dip their hands into our business is alarming.

"Yes. Big time. Did you call Dushku to let him know?"

"Yes. I'm meeting him tonight," Roman says. "I told O'Neil that I'm otherwise engaged, and that you'll come instead."

"When?"

"In four hours. He picked someplace in the industrial district. I'll send you the location."

"Okay."

"Be careful, and call me the moment you're done. I don't like this."

"Alright." I cut the line and look down at Angelina, who is still plastered to my chest, her breathing labored. Her legs still shaking. My phone pings. Must be the text from Roman. I glance at it briefly and forward it to Felix.

"I need to call Albert. We'll head home right after."

"Okay," she whispers into my chest.

I keep caressing her back as I hit the speed dial for Felix. I love this, how she feels in my arms.

"What?" Felix barks the moment the line connects.

"You're in a nice mood."

"I had a fight with Marlene."

Again? Those two need a relationship counseling.

"I'm meeting Liam O'Neil in four hours," I say as I move my hand to pet the top of Angelina's head. "I need you to access the cameras around the meeting spot and check if there's anything suspicious. I've forwarded you the location Roman sent."

"What am I looking for?"

"I'm not sure. They said they want to discuss business, but the story doesn't hold. Do you have someone in the vicinity who could make a pass closer to the meeting time?"

"Let me see the location first." There are a few seconds of silence. "Hmm. I think Little Sam's bakery is on the next block. He could have a look."

"Good. We'll be home soon."

Angelina

The ride to Sergei's house takes half an hour, but I can still feel my legs shaking the whole way back. I can't believe we had sex in a car. That *I* had sex in a car. I've only had one boyfriend, and the two times we slept together, it was in a bed, lights off, missionary position. It wasn't exactly a mind-blowing experience, but I thought it was okay. Impulsive is the farthest word to describe me, but when I felt Sergei's hands on my pussy, I ignited. I couldn't think about anything other than having him inside me, right away.

The madness only intensified when I heard him speaking with his pakhan over the phone. It felt somehow forbidden but also alluring, me riding him in his car, where anyone could see us. But when he thrust his finger into my mouth to silence me so Petrov wouldn't hear us, it pushed me over the edge.

I steal a look at Sergei. He said he needs to go to a meeting tonight, but I still feel that tingling desire between my legs. Would he object to the second round?

Sergei parks in the driveway but doesn't make a move to leave the car.

"Do you regret it?" he asks, squeezing the steering wheel. "It's okay if you do. Just tell me, and I won't touch you again."

I just stare at him. What the fuck is he talking about?

"You haven't said a word the whole drive, Angelina."

"I was . . . processing." I'm not very good with relationship stuff, or people in general. It usually takes me some time to warm up to a person. The fact that I'm so strongly attracted to someone I barely know is scary.

"Processing?" He sighs and buries his hands in his hair. "Just tell me honestly if you don't want to have anything with a mentally unstable person and . . ."

I lunge at him. There isn't a better word to describe the way I leap from my seat, straddle him, and wrap my arms around his neck.

"Angelina?"

"Just shut up," I bite out and slam my lips to his.

My dress ends up around my hips again, so my naked core is pressing directly onto his crotch, with the fabric of his pants as the only barrier between my pussy and his hardening cock. Without removing my mouth from his, I let my palms slide down his body, I reach the waistband of his pants and release his cock in haste. Sergei smiles into my mouth and, reaching his hands between our bodies, buries his finger inside me. But just as quickly as it was there, it's gone.

"We'll have to be fast." He grabs me around the waist, lifts me, and slams me down onto his hard dick.

The moment I feel him inside, my walls start clenching, and I ride him like a maniac, clutching the fabric of his shirt between my fingers. Sergei groans, then leans back a bit causing his cock to get even deeper within my pussy, filling me completely.

"Will you be late for the meeting?"

"Fuck the meeting." His hands travel up my body to my already tangled hair, gripping the strands between his fingers. I bend my head and bite at the side of his neck—hard—and feel his cock swelling inside of me. The pressure between my legs intensifies, and when his upward thrusting intensifies to a brutal pace, I feel my orgasm hit me harder than it ever has before, just as Sergei finishes with me.

I try fixing my hair and the dress in the car to make myself more presentable, but I still feel like anyone looking at me would know what we just did. As we climb the steps to the front door, I glance down at my hand clasped in Sergei's, our fingers intertwined.

"I need to take a shower and change before the meeting with the Irish," he says as we go inside.

"Okay." I nod.

Sergei bends and tilts my head up with his finger under my chin. "Processing again?"

"Kind of."

"Do your thing, then." He nods. "And, when I come back,

we can discuss the subject some more. To give you more material for processing."

I stare at him. "I doubt that my pussy would be able to handle another discussion today."

"We'll see." He presses a quick kiss on my lips and heads upstairs.

When I walk inside the kitchen, Felix is sitting at the dining table with a robust-looking laptop in front of him. I quickly straighten the front of my dress and pass my hand through my hair one more time. It feels like I have "just had sex in the car twice" tattooed onto my forehead. The fact that I don't have panties on doesn't help, either.

"Are you going to stand there all night, looking guilty as hell?" Felix asks without looking up from the laptop.

I tilt my chin up and head toward the fridge to get something to drink. "I have no idea what you're talking about."

"You two should have been here half an hour ago."

"There was a traffic jam."

"Oh?" He looks at me over the rim of his glasses. "That's what you kids call it these days?"

"What do you mean?"

He rolls his eyes. "I'm not blind, and I'm not yet senile."

I ignore his comment and walk over to stand behind him. The screen on his laptop shows a camera feed with different angles of a street. "Are those . . . traffic cameras?"

He nods. "Four traffic cameras and one ATM camera."

"How did you access those?"

"That's what I do—or did—when Sergei and I worked together. He went into the field, and I provided support from the base."

"And the other people on the team? What were their jobs?"

Felix looks up at me. "There were never other people. It was always one operative and one handler."

"He was sent on missions alone? What about backup? What if something happened and he needed help?"

"Sergei rarely needed help, Angelina." He smiles and looks down at the screen. "I missed this."

I hear the footsteps behind me and turn to find Sergei coming in. He's wearing another suit, with a black dress shirt this time.

"Anything?" he asks, reaches for the guns on the counter, and places them in a shoulder holster hidden under his jacket. He didn't have those earlier.

"Nothing so far." Felix gestures at the laptop. "Little Sam will do a pass in half an hour."

"Good." Sergei nods, takes a big rectangular box from the chair, and puts it on the table.

When he opens the lid to check the contents, I move to the side to take a peek and falter. It's a sniper's rifle. "I thought you were going to a business meeting?"

"Something about this meeting doesn't sit well with me." He reaches for the earpiece Felix passes him, and puts it in. "I'm going to do a sweep when I get there. Let me know the moment you see the Irish coming."

He closes the box with the rifle, picks it up, and looks over at me. "I'll be back in a couple of hours." He smirks, and he's gone the next moment.

I wait until I hear the front door close, then sit down on the chair next to Felix. "How come Petrov lets Sergei handle business deals? Considering his mental state."

"Because even mentally unstable Sergei does great work. And anyway, none of the people they partner with are fully sane."

"He never zones out while he's at a meeting?"

"Nope. Not at a meeting. And never in the field," he says. "He happens to overdo stuff occasionally, though."

"Yeah, I heard. He almost killed four of my father's men when they met to talk about partnering last year."

"I remember that. He was probably in a good mood that day."

"Good mood?"

Felix puts down his glasses and fixes me with his stare. "There were five of them, four bodyguards and your father. All armed. Sergei was alone. They tried to disarm him. It was very disrespectful from their side. I was pleasantly surprised when he didn't just kill them all, your father included."

"How did he manage to overpower all four of them if everyone was armed?"

"With frightening ease. Your father's men were just some hired goons with no real training."

He puts his glasses back on and turns his gaze to the screen again. "This will take a while. Go to sleep."

I most certainly don't plan on sleeping until Sergei comes back. I run upstairs to shower and change, then head back and take a seat next to Felix.

CHAPTER Thirteen

 Sergei

I FINISH ASSEMBLING THE RIFLE, PROP IT ON THE ROOF'S surface, and focus the scope on the small group of people standing by a car down the alley. There are four of them at the meeting point, and only one car.

I turn on the mic. "Felix?"

"What, no more Albert thing?"

"Albert is the guy who washes dishes," I say. "You're Felix when conducting surveillance."

"You're hilarious. What's the situation?"

"They're early. I see four of them. One car."

"I caught another car a bit further down, behind some dumpster, and two suspicious-looking guys in the side alley around the corner. I marked the locations and sent the map to your phone. Little Sam said he noticed another car doing laps around the block."

"How many people inside?" I ask.

"No idea. Tinted windows."

"Okay. Out."

I check the location markers Felix sent on my phone, then call Roman. "Where are you?"

"Home. Nina isn't feeling well. She caught some bug. We're waiting for the doc."

"What about the meeting with Dushku?"

"I sent Kostya."

"Dushku doesn't like the kid, you know that."

"Yeah well, he'll have to manage. Fucking DEA busted into Ural an hour ago. They're combing the place. I sent Maxim to go help Pavel. Dimitri and Ivan went to Baykal in case the DEA decides to visit it as well. There wasn't anyone else available."

What an unusual coincidence. I look down at the Irish. "Which car did Kostya take?"

"Mine. He crashed his again, two days ago."

"I need you to call Kostya," I say, watching the men down below. "Tell him to turn around and get back to the mansion. Right now. And double the security."

"Why?"

"O'Neil is here with three more men, waiting for me. But Fitzgerald is not. O'Neil never conducts business deals without him. There are also two other cars out of view, and some men hiding in the back alley."

"Ambush?"

"Yes. This one's for me. He probably has someone following Kostya's car, too, thinking it's you inside. Call him right away, or they'll kill him."

"Fuck!"

The line goes dead. I continue watching the men. At one moment O'Neil reaches for his phone and speaks to someone briefly. Five minutes later, my phone vibrates.

"Two cars intercepted Kostya at the underpass," Roman says. "The car is abandoned there, with tires shot out."

I take a deep breath and grit my teeth. "Call Felix. He's already connected to the traffic cameras. I need to know where they took him. I'll clean house here and go back to gear up."

"You're not going alone. You hear me?"

"Call Felix," I bark, cut the call, and put my eye back on the scope.

I off O'Neil first. One shot, right to the chest. The man on his right is next. They're both on the ground before the other two even realize what's happening. The last two run for the car. I kill one, but the last man manages to duck out of view.

Getting up with my rifle, I walk to the other side of the roof and set up position again, waiting for the last guy to try getting into the car. He does exactly that. When he's inside, I send the last bullet through the open window, right to his head. Four down. Six more to go.

I put the rifle back into the case and look at my watch. Twenty minutes is the most I can afford to spend here. I set the timer, take out my handgun, and head back inside the building.

The two guys in the side alley are easy to dispatch—they don't even see me coming—but the last four are going to be more difficult to deal with because they're sitting inside a locked, and probably armored, car behind the dumpster. There isn't enough time to bother with the gun. A look at my watch. Five minutes left. Fuck. I run across the street to my car, stowing the sniper inside the trunk and retrieving a small grenade launcher from the hidden compartment. Luca said its accuracy is impeccable. Good thing the Irish picked a deserted location for the meeting.

I run toward the corner, aim, and fire. A few seconds later, the car with the Irish explodes, sending a magnificent thunder into the night.

Angelina

"Got them," Felix mumbles next to me.

He's been switching through traffic cameras' recordings for the last forty minutes, looking for the car that left the underpass with Kostya inside. I tried to track what Felix was seeing on the screen, but he's too quick. I barely managed to catch a glimpse of the two black SUVs here and there as he flipped between the video feeds.

The front door bursts open, and Sergei runs across the living room, heading toward the stairs that lead to the basement.

"You have them?" he shouts.

"Yes. An abandoned house south of the city. I'll send you the GPS location."

"What's going on?" I ask.

"Sergei is going to get Kostya."

"Now?"

"The Irish will try to extract as much information as they can from him, then they will kill him. It has to be within the next hour or so," Felix says and nods.

"Who's going with him?"

"He'll pick up Dimitri on the way, but he'll be staying with the car. Sergei is going in alone."

"What?" I widen my eyes at him. "You don't know how many people are there! He can get killed!"

"There couldn't be more than six or seven people in those cars. They probably don't have anyone at the location. This wasn't planned. They expected Roman, and would have just killed him if he'd been in that car."

"It's still seven against one!"

"We can't risk sending anyone else, Angelina. If the Irish see them coming, they'll kill Kostya on the spot."

The sound of quick footsteps reaches me, and Sergei rushes into the kitchen a moment later. I look him over, my eyes scanning the bulletproof vest over a long-sleeved black T-shirt, black tactical pants with leg holsters holding knives, extra magazines, and a gun, as well as two more guns in shoulder holsters. He looks like he's going to war.

"We're good?" he asks.

"Yes." Felix looks up at him. "Don't die."

Sergei nods and turns to me. He doesn't say anything, only watches me for a few seconds, then reaches up and traces a line down my cheek with his finger. I open my mouth to say something, but he turns away and marches to the front door. All I can do is stare at his back as he leaves.

"One man in the parked car down the street. Two by the door," Sergei's low voice comes through the headphones that Felix gave me. "Three more inside the house. With Kostya."

"Is he alive?" Felix asks.

"Yes. But he's beaten up pretty bad. Tell Roman to have the doc wait for us at the mansion."

"Doc is already there."

"Good. I'm going in."

For a few minutes, the only thing I can hear is Sergei's breathing. Then, suddenly, there's a choking sound that lasts for a few seconds. I strain my ears, trying to catch anything else, but the only sound coming though once again is barely audible breathing.

Rustling. Something hits the ground. A short silence, then someone starts panting and a choking sound comes again.

I grab the edge of the table in front of me, trying to control my own erratic breaths.

Distant voices. Three gunshots in quick succession. Someone screams. Yelling. Several gunshots. Sergei cursing. A thud. Gunfire again, followed by shouting. Running feet. A single gunshot. A sound of something breaking. Two more gunshots. Then, silence, broken only by the sound of heavy breathing.

"Kostya!" Sergei's voice. "*Davay. Poshli.*"

Grunting. A few Russian curses.

"I have him," Sergei says into the mic. "Tell Dimitri to bring the car around the front. The kid weighs a ton, and he's barely conscious."

I let out a breath and close my eyes, listening to Felix as he calls Dimitri, then someone else. I don't pay attention to what's said because I'm engrossed in the sound of Sergei's slightly labored breathing. Is he okay? He doesn't sound that well. Was he shot? I look at Felix who's still on the phone, but he doesn't look concerned.

I unmute the speaker on my headphones.

"Sergei? Are you okay?" I ask.

He doesn't say anything. There's a sound of an approaching car, then, the screech of tires.

"Sergei?" I try again.

After a few moments of silence, I get a dry reply, "I'm okay. Dimitri is here, I have to go."

I hear the car door opening, rustling, and a few more curses, then the door bangs closed. The audio feed disconnects.

Sergei

Thirty minutes earlier

There's some kind of shed a hundred yards from the house where they're holding Kostya. I would prefer something closer, in case I have to carry the kid out in haste, but it'll do. After parking the car behind the shed, I take the black beanie from my pocket and put it on. Going on a night mission with hair as light as mine uncovered, is just asking for a bullet to the head.

"I'm coming with you," Dimitri says from the passenger's seat and takes out his gun.

"If you dare leave this car," I say as I'm pulling on my gloves, "I'm going to knock you out and dump you into the trunk."

"Damn it, Sergei."

I look up, right into his eyes. "Stay. Put."

Dimitri glares at me, then throws the gun onto the dash. Good.

After leaving the car, I cross the wide patch of grass to the backyard. It takes me longer than I'd like to reach the fence because I have to make sure not to step on the junk scattered around the ground and alert the Irish. I do a wide circle around the house and the yard to see where the men are located, then get closer to take a look at the room where they're keeping Kostya.

There are three goons inside with Kostya. They have him strapped to a chair in the corner. Two of the guys are standing to the side, and the third is in the process of rearranging Kostya's internal organs with his fists. The side of Kostya's face is swollen and bloody, and one of his arms is hanging in an unnatural angle. The kid looks awful.

I retrace my steps to the front of the house, crouch behind a bush, and update Felix on the status at the location. With that done, I head toward the front gate, hugging the side of the house to stay out of view, focused on the man inside the parked car. The guy is so engrossed in porn playing on his phone, he doesn't even register when I slide into the backseat and wrap my arm around his neck. I'm positive the guy is dead, but I snap his neck before leaving the car anyway. Better safe than sorry.

Keeping to the shadows, I move in closer and then creep along the wall toward the two guys at the front door. They're smoking and chatting, and their guns are secured inside the holsters as if they don't have a care in the world. One stands with his back to me, so I focus on the other and take out one of my throwing knives. They might not be a good choice if you want to dispatch someone, but they certainly make a hell of a distraction. After gauging the distance, I swing and let the knife fly. It finds its target, hitting the guy dead center in his neck.

It takes me exactly three seconds to reach them. Using my

bowie knife, I kill the guy facing away from me first. The idiot is so focused on the blade protruding from his friend's neck that he hasn't even reached for his weapon. Letting the body fall, I slash at the neck of the other man, finishing off the job.

Now, the harder part.

If the situation was different, I would have picked off all six of the Irish, one by one, with my sniper rifle, but having Kostya's life on the line changes things. I can't afford to alert any of them to my presence, or they'll kill the kid before I get to him. It's either stealth or guns blazing. The last three guys are in the room with Kostya, so there is no way to sneak in and neutralize them individually. I'll need to barge in and kill all of them in one fell swoop.

Taking out my gun, I step inside the house and traverse the narrow hallway. The door at the end is ajar, the captors' voices reaching me as I approach. When I reach it, I lift my gun and kick the door. I send three bullets into the first man I see, then turn on the one raising his gun at Kostya. I shoot, aiming for his head. The asshole moves at just that moment, and my bullet finds the wall instead. I fire at him twice more, hitting my mark, but gasp and stumble as I get hit square in the chest. It was likely a low caliber, so I manage to recover a split second later. I take a breath, ignore the pain, and shoot at the only remaining guy. My bullet strikes him in the center of his head, and his body falls backward, crashing over a coffee table.

I enter the room, put a bullet in the head of each lifeless body for good measure, then rush to Kostya and cut his restraints.

"Kostya!" I wrap my arm around his back. "*Davay. Poshli.*"

Even semiconscious, he manages to stand up, grunting

in the process. I put his good arm around my neck and start dragging him out.

We're at the front of the house, waiting for Dimitri, when I hear the voice in my earpiece and my blood goes ice-cold.

"Sergei? Are you okay?"

I shut my eyes, wanting to hit something. She's been listening the entire time.

Angelina

Sergei arrives an hour later. The moment I see the front door open, I leap up from the couch where I've been waiting. Instead of coming over, he just glances in my direction and heads for the stairs. I stand in the middle of the living room, staring at his retreating form, wondering what the hell is going on. I make a decision then. If he wants to be left alone, it will have to be some other time, because I need to know he's okay.

I reach the top of the stairs just in time to see him going into his bedroom. When I make it inside the room, he's nowhere to be seen, but the water is running in the bathroom.

"Sergei?" I call, and when I don't receive an answer, I approach and open the door.

Sergei is standing in front of the sink, his head is bent, and his hands are gripping the edge of the counter so hard his knuckles have turned white.

"Felix shouldn't have let you listen to the audio feed," he says without raising his head.

I take a couple of steps forward and place my hand on his. "Why?"

"Because I don't like the idea of you listening while I'm killing people, Angelina."

He still won't look at me. Instead, he focuses intently on the sink, his jaw clenched tight. I turn off the water, then place my hand on his cheek and slowly turn his head toward me.

"Hearing or seeing people being killed is nothing new to me, Sergei." I brush the back of my hand down the side of his face. "You're covered in blood."

"It's not mine."

"Good." I nod and start unstrapping his vest.

As he pulls the vest over his head, a hiss escapes his mouth. "Shit," he mumbles, grabs his shirt, and pulls it off, revealing a wicked-looking red mark nestled between the black lines of his tattoos.

"Sergei!" I gasp and lean in to inspect it. "Is this from a gunshot?"

"It's just a bruise. The vest stopped the bullet."

I reach out and lightly brush the injured skin with the tip of my finger. He could have died. How could they let him go in there alone?

There's a soft touch on my chin as he takes it between his fingers and tilts my face up. "It's just soft tissue trauma. It happens."

He says this as if being shot is not a big deal. What if he hadn't been wearing the bulletproof vest? What if it had been a bullet capable of piercing the vest? I look into his eyes, which are watching me, grip his face between my palms, and press my lips to his. He doesn't respond for a second or two, but then he grabs me around the waist, pressing me to him as his lips start attacking mine.

The arm around my middle tightens and lifts me onto the

countertop next to the sink. Sergei's lips vanish from mine, and I open my eyes to find him looking at me with his head cocked to the side.

"Do you know what you're getting yourself into, Angelina?" he asks, and I watch with wide eyes as he reaches for the knife strapped to his thigh.

I follow the huge blade as he moves it to my chest and places the slightly curved tip under the first button of my shirt. There are a few dark stains on its sleek metal surface that look like dried blood. Is he trying to scare me off?

"Yes." Tilting my head up, I look right into his light eyes. I might look mousy, but I'm not easily scared. People who are willing to kill in order to protect don't frighten me. I'm only afraid of those who hurt others simply to enjoy their pain.

I reach out and wrap my fingers around the hand holding the knife. The button flies away, clattering onto the floor.

He moves the blade lower, hooking the tip under the next target. "Are you sure about that?"

I nod, and the second button falls to the floor. The third follows soon after, and I sit, unmoving, as he continues cutting them off until they are all gone. Taking a deep breath, I shrug the shirt off and let it fall. Sergei's lips curve upward, and I suck in a breath when the cold blade lightly presses against the center of my chest.

"I like this bra," I choke out.

"Me, too," he says, hooking his finger under the fabric that's holding the cups together, and moves the tip of the knife up. "But I prefer it off."

He cuts the thin piece of fabric, and my pussy clenches, drenching my panties.

Without removing my eyes from his, I discard the ruined

piece of lace, letting it fall away to join my shirt, and lean back. Sergei drops the knife into the sink, then slips his fingers into the waistband of my jeans, and bends his head until his face is right in front of mine.

"There will be no going back after this, baby," he says.

Yes, I guess there won't be. Supporting myself with my palms on the counter, I lift my ass as he slides my pants down my legs. I expected him to remove my panties next, but instead, he reaches for the knife again, hooks the tip under the string, and cuts it.

"Do you enjoy ruining my underwear?"

"Immensely." He smirks, then repeats the action on the other side. The last piece of the fabric covering me falls off, leaving me completely bare, on display under the bright fluorescent light for him. If it was any other man, I would be nervous. Not with Sergei. He's already seen me at my worst, so I don't feel the need to hide from him.

Keeping his eyes glued to mine, he starts unstrapping the holsters from around his thighs, letting the weapons clang to the floor one after the other. A gun. Several extra magazines. Another knife. Finally, he removes his pants and boxers, and stands before me in all his naked glory. As I watch all that hard tight muscle, raw and impeccably defined, a realization dawns. His body is beautiful, but it's not just for show. Just like the guns and knives he discarded, Sergei's body is a weapon, honed to perfection and capable of ending a person's life with minimum of effort—just like I witnessed tonight.

He moves closer and grabs at the back of my neck with his left hand, sliding his right down my spine, and pulls me forward until the tip of his hard cock presses at my core. I should be concerned with the fact he's just ended several lives with the same hands holding me now. There are splatters of dried blood all over his arms and face. But I'm not. Instead, I wrap my legs around his waist and revel in the feel of his cock sliding into me. It's too big and I gasp as my walls strain, stretching to accommodate his size. I'm still a little sore from earlier, but I don't care. Neither of us moves for a few moments, as we stare into each other's eyes.

This feels different somehow. Back in the car, it was just two people succumbing to sexual attraction and acting on it. But this . . . this is something else.

Until tonight, I didn't quite grasp who Sergei Belov actually is. I listened as he killed six armed men, quickly and efficiently, with no hesitation. Now, I know. I'm falling in love with a cold-blooded killer.

Sergei

Hypnotized. My cock feels like it's going to explode, but I don't move. Angelina's unblinking eyes, staring directly into mine, have me utterly hypnotized. There's no fear in them. No reluctance. People rarely look me in the eyes. If they do, most quickly turn their heads away, as if afraid of what they may see when they look too closely. Her hand rests on my shoulder, nails piercing my skin as she squeezes it while simultaneously tightening her legs around my waist and pulling me even closer.

I let my fingers trail along her back and grasp a handful of her hair, tilting her head up. She shudders and bites her bottom lip, closing her eyes.

I pull out of her, almost completely, and lightly tug her hair. "Eyes on me, baby."

I need her to look at me. The moment her eyes open, I thrust inside her with all my might. Angelina moans, clutching at my shoulders, as I bury myself in her to the hilt.

"Faster," she mewls.

"No." I smile and slide out, only to push inside again, slower this time. The sound of her panting—music to my ears. The expression on her face is priceless, something between elation and frustration. I let go of her hair and cup her chin, still moving in and out as slowly as I can, and devour Angelina's lips. She tastes like honey and sin, and my control vanishes. I grab her ass with my left hand and slam into her, holding our mouths together as our breaths mix. Angelina's hands wrap around my upper arms, squeezing as if her life depends on it, and I pound into her again and again. She moans, closing her eyes. No.

"Eyes, Angelina," I bark and latch onto her chin again. "I need you to look at me."

Her hands move up until they rest on either side of my face, and she looks at me the way she always does—like she sees *me*, not someone they send in when stuff needs to be destroyed or people eliminated. Not the unhinged man everyone fears will kill them if they look at him the wrong way. Just . . . me.

"I'm keeping you, lisichka," I say against her lips and slam in her again. "You're mine."

Angelina moans as tremors rock her body, and I keep pounding into her until I find my own release. Not even for a second does she take her eyes off mine.

"I need a shower," Sergei says against my mouth, then bites my lip. "I have blood all over me."

I sigh, still coming down from the high. "Would you mind company?"

"Nope."

His palms land on my arms and slide down, then move to my waist. He lowers me off the counter and entwines his fingers with mine. His eyes are hooded with lingering arousal as his grip on my hand remains tight. He draws me into the shower and turns the handle. The stream cascades over him, rivulets trailing down his face and body, washing away the blood. The water at his feet is pink, and I am mesmerized as it swirls before disappearing down the drain. When I look up, Sergei's eyes regard me. Waiting. I take a step forward and join him under the spray, my feet next to his in a mix of blood and water.

He raises an eyebrow. "You could have waited for the blood to wash away."

"I could have," I say looking into his eyes.

"It doesn't bother you?"

I look down at the water around my feet. There's still a pale pink tint to it. "No, not particularly."

He reaches with his hand and moves a few strands of hair that are plastered to my cheeks. "You are a strange breed."

"I'm not," I say and reach for the body wash. "I'm probably the most boring person I know."

I watch as he takes my chin between his fingers and tilts my head up.

"You are the farthest thing from boring, baby."

"Your brother said I look like a librarian."

"I have no idea how a librarian is supposed to look, but if it's like this . . ." His free hand rests on my shoulder and travels down my chest, squeezing my breast, then moves lower along my stomach, and finally stops between my legs. "Then, librarians are mind-blowingly sexy little things."

He dips his head and presses his lips to mine while his hand circles around to my behind. "With the sweetest, perky asses," he says into my mouth and slaps my butt lightly.

"If you say so." I smile, then yelp when he bites my lip.

"I do."

I smirk and squeeze a little of the body wash onto my palm.

Sergei groans. "Not the strawberry."

I look down at my hand and see that I grabbed one of mine. Smiling deviously, I squeeze out some more. As I'm washing his chest, being gentle around the spot where the bullet hit him, I take a closer look at the tattoos covering his front. Most are macabre scenes, done in great detail. Here and there, however, nestled between numerous geometric patterns and mythological creatures, are words written in Russian.

I trace my finger along the tail of a winged snake on his breastbone and follow it to his shoulder. Sergei turns around, giving me his back, and I continue along the creature's body that ends over his shoulder blade in a giant head with gaping jaws. I've noticed only one scar on the front of Sergei's body, a short horizontal line at the side of his neck, but there are several on his back. One round mark near the snake's head on his shoulder, and one more on his hip. I brush each one with my fingers, then lean forward and place a kiss on his upper arm. There is a sharp intake of breath, and the next moment, I'm pressed to the wall with Sergei's mouth devouring mine, and his hard cock throbbing against my stomach.

"That didn't take long." I brush my hand down his length. "Are we trying to break some record? Because I'm not sure I can keep this pace."

"Don't worry. Stamina comes with practice." He turns off the water, takes a towel from the shelf, and puts it around my shoulders. After wrapping me up, he lifts me in his arms and carries me out of the bathroom to bed.

"This feels familiar," I say and bury my face into the crook of his neck. "You smell differently this time, though."

"And whose fault is that?"

Smiling, I lick his neck, then bite the skin there slightly. "I wasn't complaining."

Laying me down on the bed, he climbs above me. "Now, it's my turn to taste."

Instead of leaning in to taste my neck as I expected, he moves down my body, takes my legs and places them over his shoulders, and I watch as he lowers his head and licks my pussy.

"Perfection," he mumbles, then laps it a few more times, making me gasp. He sucks on my clit, and tremors overtake my body. I want him to continue, but at the same time, I feel like I'm going to implode if he doesn't get inside me again. When he adds a finger, I whimper and grab at his hair, as my core shudders. Sergei removes his mouth from my pussy, and I groan in frustration, but in the next instant, his cock fills me completely. His body weight settles on top of me, and his heart pounds against mine. He wraps an arm around me and caresses my cheek with his other palm. I pant and hold his gaze as he drives into me.

My pussy is rubbed raw, but I don't care. Every thrust, every ache, every time his cock stretches my walls feels like a proof of life. I was so afraid for him tonight. I will never forget those twenty minutes. I'm so sick of watching everyone I care about die.

With one hand clutching him for all I'm worth, I bring my other up to cover his on my cheek. My eyes prickle. He's here. He's alive. Sergei impales me again, burying his cock to the hilt. His heartbeat speeds. Another thrust. Alive. Alive. Alive.

Chapter
fourteen

WORDS WHISPERED IN RUSSIAN. A MOVEMENT next to me. More words, faster and slightly louder. I open my eyes, still a bit groggy as sleep refuses to release its hold, and it takes me a few seconds to register where I am. The morning light bathes the room in a soft glow, and the only thing I hear is Sergei's mumbling. I turn around and find him lying on his back next to me, jaw set in a hard line and eyes closed tight. I sit up in the bed and press my palm lightly to his cheek.

"Sergei?"

His eyes snap open at the same time as his hand shoots up and wraps around my throat. I gasp, grab his wrist with both hands, and pull, but it doesn't get me anywhere.

"Dasha!" Sergei sneers, his face an image of hatred.

There's no time to think about who Dasha is, because even in scarce light, I can see that his eyes are vacant. I suck in my breath and will my body to stay still. He's not hurting me, but I'd be lying if I said that having his huge hand wrapped around my neck wasn't slightly alarming.

"Sergei, it's me. It's Angelina," I say in a calm voice.

I let go of his wrist, place my palm on his cheek again, and very slowly start moving my hand to the center of his face.

"Sergei. Please come back, big guy." I trail a finger down his nose. "I'm fascinated with your nose, you know that?"

He blinks.

"That's good," I say, and glide the tip of my finger down his nose again. "Come back, Sergei."

"Lisichka?" he whispers.

"Yup. Your bed hijacker."

I watch as he takes a deep breath, moves his gaze to the hand that's still holding on to my neck, and tenses.

"Jesus fuck." He lets go of my neck like he's been burned and jumps up off the bed. He staggers backward until he hits the wall, then lowers himself onto the floor, staring at me the whole time.

"I fell asleep." The way he says it, it sounds like it's the most atrocious thing he could have done. "I can't believe I let myself fall asleep next to you."

"Sergei . . ."

"I could have killed you." He buries his hands in his hair, closes his eyes, and bangs the back of his head against the wall. "I'm so sorry, baby."

I wrap the blanket around me, leave the bed, and come to kneel on the floor in front of him.

"Don't!" I cup his face with my hands. "It's my fault.

Felix warned me not to touch you when you're asleep. I forgot."

"It's not your fault that I'm fucked up," he says. "I'm taking you to a hotel today. You're not safe with me around."

"I'm not going to a hotel."

"Okay. Then, I'll go."

I press my lips together. "You're not going anywhere, either."

"Angelina—"

"No. We're both staying here. And we will find a way to work around this."

His head snaps up and he stares at me with his eyes wide. "Are you crazy? I almost choked you to death, for God's sake."

"You were just holding me away from you. Next time, I'll wait until you're awake before touching you."

"There won't be a next time, Angelina. I'm not making the same mistake and endangering you ever again."

"I woke you up in the middle of a nightmare, Sergei. You thought I was a threat. And still, you didn't hurt me."

"I could have." He shakes his head. "You need to stay away from me."

I lean forward until my nose touches his. "Not happening. Let's get back to bed."

"No. I'm going to the other room. There's no way I'll be able to sleep after what happened, but just in case."

"Okay." I nod. "I'm taking the pillow and coming with you. And just so you know, I hate sleeping on the floor. I went camping once when I was in third grade. One of the worst experiences of my life, and that's a very competitive list."

"You are not sleeping on the floor, Angelina."

"The bed it is, then. I'm glad we agree on that." I take his hand and get up. "Come. Please."

He lets me pull him up, and reluctantly follows across the room. Climbing into bed, I scoot over to make room for him and pat the pillow next to my head. Sergei watches me, his face grim, then sits on the bed with his back to me and hangs his head, staring at the floor between his feet. It's obvious he isn't planning to lie down. I shift to sit behind him with my legs on either side of his hips, wrapping my arms around his chest. Resting my left palm just over his heart, I put my cheek on his back.

Sergei takes a deep breath and covers my hand with his. "I'm fucked up, Angelina. Seriously fucked up."

"That's okay. I like you just the way you are." I close my eyes and nuzzle his back with my nose. "Who's Dasha?"

His body goes still, but the heartbeat under my palm picks up. For a long time, he doesn't say anything. He doesn't move a muscle, and I'm certain my question will stay unanswered.

But then, he starts talking. "Dasha was my wife," he whispers, and my eyes snap open.

"We met by accident," he continues, "or that's what I believed at the time. Six years ago. She was a few years older than me, a waitress in a coffee shop I frequented. Shy. Slightly unsure of herself. She was Russian. Here on a work visa, trying to get her papers." He scoffs. "I was young. Stupid. I believed the farce. And, I liked her. Felix checked her background, of course. It seemed solid. When I told him I was going to marry her so she could get her green card, he went ballistic. At least at first, but then he said it might be good for me to have someone. I wasn't in a good place then."

"So, you married her?"

"Yes. She moved in with me. It was nice for the first few months." He squeezes my fingers. "Then, she started asking me about work. Small things, at first. Where I've been. What did I do exactly. I told her that I worked for the government, and I couldn't share any work-related information. She started pressing more and more, and got frustrated when I didn't say anything."

He takes a deep breath. "One night, I came home from a long mission. I was tired and sleep deprived. We were together for six months at that time, but I'd stopped sleeping in our bed two weeks earlier, and I planned on asking her to move out. I crashed on the sofa. Something woke me up later. It wasn't a noise or anything like that. Dasha was too well trained to let herself get noticed. Maybe it was an instinct. One second, I was deep asleep, and the next, my eyes snapped open to find her looming over me with one of my knives at my throat."

He raises his hand and places it on the right side of his neck, over the horizontal scar I noticed while we were showering.

"I hesitated only for a moment, enough for her to start slicing my skin, but then my training kicked in. I grabbed her and snapped her neck." He shakes his head. "The next morning, Felix pulled some strings and managed to run her prints through the international database. She was an operative for the Russian government. We found a secret email account on her phone where she was receiving her orders. The last communication thread showed her reporting that I wouldn't talk, and asking for permission to pull out. The reply said to kill me so I don't blow her cover."

Dear God. "Did you love her?"

"I don't know. Maybe." He looks up toward the door. He hasn't looked at me even once since he started telling me about his wife. "Do you understand what could have happened earlier?"

I kiss his back. "Yes."

"Good."

He nods and starts getting up, but I squeeze my arms and wrap my legs around him. "It doesn't mean that you're going to the other room."

"Baby . . ."

"You are"—I kiss his left shoulder—"staying here"— another kiss on his arm—"with me."

I let my hands travel upward, hooking him under the arms, then shift my entire weight to the side. He leans with me until we're both lying on the bed.

"Your demons don't scare me," I whisper in his ear. "You forget, I was raised in a hyena's den, Sergei. I might be cultured. My father made sure I got the best education, but I still spent most of my life surrounded by men who were either bad or crazy."

I take his hand and place his palm on the side of my thigh, over the scar he once asked me about. "I didn't fall off a tree. I was kidnapped when I was seven. A bullet caught me when my father's man was carrying me out of a shed where my kidnapper kept me for ransom."

He sucks in a breath, and I place a kiss on his nape.

Then, I lift my right hand, spreading my fingers in front of his face to show him the long faded scar across my palm. "One of the men at the compound tried raping me when I was thirteen. I cut my hand as I was trying to take his knife from him."

"Did he?" Sergei asks, his voice barely audible. "Did he rape you?"

"Nope. He was too drunk. I took his gun, which he left on the nightstand, and shot him in his filthy penis. He screamed like a pig being slaughtered."

Sergei turns around so he's facing me, and buries his hand in my hair, amazement evident in his eyes. "You know how to shoot a gun?"

I chuckle. "Everybody at the compound knows how to use a gun."

"Aren't you full of surprises, Miss Sandoval?"

"It's survival, I guess." I shrug. "Even my nana knows how to shoot."

I smile, but it's sad. It hurts to think about her, to wonder if she's still alive. "Can you remind your pakhan about his promise?"

"What promise?"

"He said he'll try to get some info about her. I'm not sure if Diego hurt her when he found out she helped me escape."

"I will, baby." He leans forward and places a kiss on my forehead. "Go back to sleep."

"You'll stay?"

I feel his chest rising under my palm as he takes a deep breath. "I'll stay."

Smiling, I bury my face into his neck and, inhaling his

wild, familiar, comforting scent, I close my eyes and revel in the feel of his arms enveloping me, and his breath in my hair. He's scared that he might unintentionally hurt me, but the fact is, I don't remember the last time I felt as protected as I do in Sergei's embrace.

"Don't you dare leave this bed," I mumble and let myself drift off to sleep.

Sergei

I wait until Angelina falls asleep, then get up, head to my closet to put on some clothes, and rummage through the drawers until I find my stash of cigarettes. Taking the half-full pack and collecting my phone on the way, I leave the room and whistle for Mimi, who rushes up the stairs a couple of seconds later. I point to the bedroom door and give her the order to guard, then descend the stairs and go outside. I fish out the ashtray hidden under the first step, take a seat on the porch, and call Roman.

"How's the kid?" I ask.

"Christ, Sergei!" he whispers-yells into the phone. "It's five in the morning."

There are some rustling sounds, probably him heading into another room, then a door closing. "He'll be okay. Olga and Valentina have been busy being his nursemaids the whole night."

"Do they know he's slept with both of them?"

"Well, based on the scene I walked into when I went to check up on him earlier, they most certainly do. I found him sprawled out in bed, with Valentina on his right and Olga on his left. The three of them snuggled together."

"Nice."

"You know, sometimes I wonder if there's anyone who isn't crazy under this roof." He huffs. "How are you?"

"I'm okay." I light up a cigarette and take a big inhale. "What are we going to do about the Irish?"

"I had Yuri and Dimitri burn down that bar of theirs. And, I sent a message to Patrick, since I assume he's the one who will take over now."

"Oh? What was the message?"

"They have two days to leave Chicago. Everyone who stays will end up dead."

"You think he'll do it?"

"Fitzgerald is a coward. They will leave."

"Good." I lean my back against the railing and take another drag. "Roman?"

"Yes?"

"Thank you," I say. "For putting up with me."

There are a few moments of silence from the other side before he answers. "You don't have to thank me for anything, Sergei. You're good at what you do for the Bratva."

"Yeah. When I don't blow up stuff or kill people I shouldn't." I snort.

"Well, there is that." He yawns. "Varya always puts too much salt in the soup. Kostya crashes cars every month. I guess nobody's perfect."

I burst out laughing. Leave it to Roman to pull a parallel between my case and Varya's cooking. "Phone me tomorrow to let me know how it went with the Irish."

I cut the call and drop my head back on the post behind

me, closing my eyes. I hoped calling Roman would distract me from what happened with Angelina earlier. It didn't. And I have no idea what to do with her. Even though I know it would be for the best, the mere thought of sending her away makes me want to go on a rampage.

"Sergei?"

I open my eyes and find Angelina standing at the front door, wrapped in a blanket, and watching me with concern. Her feet are bare, her hair is tangled and sticking out in all directions, and she has sleep creases on her left cheek. Mimi is six feet behind her, but when she notices me, she barks and turns away, probably heading to the living room to sleep.

"You'll catch a cold," I say.

Angelina shrugs, covers the distance that separates us in a few quick steps, and sits down between my legs, leaning back on my chest.

"That's an awful habit." She nods toward my hand holding a cigarette.

"Does it bother you?"

"Nope. I'm just saying."

I extinguish the cigarette and move the ashtray away.

"Is everything okay?" she asks.

"Yeah." I wrap my arms around her and bury my nose in her hair, inhaling her flowery scent. "You?"

"I miss my dad," she whispers, looking at the dawn sky. "It's strange. We never spent much time together, especially in the last couple of years. I only went to Mexico during summer vacation, and it was usually only for a week or two. I tried to stay away from that madness as much as possible. Still, I miss him."

"You weren't close?"

"I wouldn't say we weren't close." She shrugs. "We didn't see each other often, but he called every Sunday evening like clockwork. He was very proud of me for going to college. No one in my family had higher education."

"Was it your dad who insisted you move to the US?"

"Yes. His main goal was to get me away from the cartel, and he didn't want me coming back to Mexico every summer, but I needed to see him and my nana at least once a year. They were my only family."

I move my head to the side of her neck and nuzzle her with my nose, loving the way she tilts up to give me more access. "And your mom?"

"She died when I was little. Cancer. I don't even remember her. It was always just my dad and Nana Guadalupe."

"We'll get her out," I say and squeeze my arm around her waist. "I promise."

Angelina exhales and leans her head back on my shoulder. I don't think she believes me, but I vow to myself I'll get her nana here, no matter the consequences.

"Sergei?" she whispers. "Where do you go when you zone out?"

I go still for a moment, caught unprepared by her question, then put my chin on her shoulder and stare at the horizon. "I'm not sure how to explain," I say. "It's like I'm here, but only partially. I can hear and see what's happening around me, but I can't control my actions. You should stay away from me when I'm in that state. I don't want to hurt you, even unintentionally."

Angelina turns to look at me, her eyes finding mine and holding my gaze as she places her hand on the side of my face. "I don't think you could ever hurt me, Sergei. Intentionally or not." She tilts her head up until her lips press softly against mine. "I'm not afraid of you, big guy."

"You should be, Angelina," I say into her mouth. "You never saw me lose it completely, baby. If you did, you would have run away and never looked back."

"Is that what other people do when you lose it? Run away?"

"If they're clever, yes."

Angelina smiles and places the tip of her finger on my nose, tracing the line down the ridge until she reaches my mouth. "Well, I don't plan on running, Sergei. In fact, I plan on coming even closer and holding you until you come back from wherever you go." Her mouth finds mine, and as her lips explore, I forget about the blood and the killings for a moment. The rage I've lived with constantly for so long recedes.

CHAPTER fifteen

📚 Angelina 📚

"WHERE ARE WE GOING?" I ASK AS WE'RE walking toward the bike.

"You'll see." Sergei smirks.

I narrow my eyes at him and reach for the bag he's carrying. "What's inside?"

He moves the bag out of my reach. "No peeking."

"Are we going on a picnic? Did you pack ketchup?"

"We are not going on a fucking picnic." He straps the bag to the back of his bike and passes me the helmet. "Why would I take you on a picnic?"

"Because girls like that?"

"Bullshit. No girl wants to sit on grass and eat off a plastic plate while trying to shoo away the ants and flies."

"Well, when you put it that way." I shrug and get on the bike behind him.

Sergei starts the engine, and I quickly wrap my arms around his waist, clutching him with a mad grip. That first tug when he takes off is the worst. Even after the numerous times he's taken me for a ride, I still need a couple of minutes to adjust to the idea being on the back of a motorcycle. I can't help it. The thought that vehicles with two wheels shouldn't exist won't leave me. But then, I remember it's Sergei driving, so I relax and let myself enjoy the adrenaline surge.

I have seen him ride the bike alone. It's fucking madness. I keep thinking he'll crash into something. When I saw him doing that idiotic thing on one wheel last week, I almost had a heart attack. He never tries that when I'm with him, though, thank God.

We drive along the highway for about forty minutes before he takes a turn onto a side road, and then to a narrow dirt path leading between the fields. I'm convinced we're lost when he slows down and parks. There's nothing around except grass for miles.

"Are we lost?" I ask when I remove my helmet.

"Nope." He smiles, takes me around the waist, and lifts me off the bike. "Let's go."

He unstraps the bag from the back, takes my hand in his free one, and leads me across the field on our right. A hundred yards in, we reach a roughly made wooden table, standing in the middle of nowhere. A bit farther, I notice several metal stands with paddles on each side, placed at varying distances from the table. Practice targets.

"I didn't know what you liked," Sergei says and puts the bag onto the table.

I watch with wide eyes as he starts taking out different handguns and lining them on the wooden surface. Two Glocks. A Sig Sauer, smaller model. A Beretta. And two more pistols—I don't recognize the manufacturer, but they look like military issue.

169

"Take your pick." He nods toward the assortment of weapons.

I raise an eyebrow. "You brought me to a shooting practice?"

"It's better than picnic." He smiles. "And I want to see you shoot."

I narrow my eyes at him. "You didn't believe me when I said I know how to use a gun?"

"Of course, I believed you." He leans down and presses his lips to mine. "But I want to see if you can actually hit something."

I smile into his lips. "Okay."

He turns me around to face the table and stands behind me. "How about the Sig? That one would be the easiest for you to use. Do you know how to turn the safety off?"

He's so sweet. "I don't like Sigs." I reach out and take the Glock 19. It's relatively light and has a dual recoil system. I check the magazine. "I'll do a round of six. And then you. We'll see who'll end up with more hits."

Sergei bursts out laughing. "Deal."

The first target is rather close, so I decide to go for the second one. Coming around the table, I lift the gun and aim for the top left paddle. My first shot is a hit. I make the next three too, then miss with the fifth one. Crap. The sixth one strikes true. I put the safety on, lower the gun, and turn around to find Sergei gaping at me.

"Well, it looks like I managed to hit something, huh?" I smirk.

He stares at me for a few heartbeats, then grabs me around the waist so suddenly, the gun falls from my hand.

Lifting me up, he plasters me to his body and our mouths collide.

Violent, desperate kisses, then . . . "There is nothing sexier than a girl who knows how to handle a gun." He takes my lower lip between his teeth, biting it lightly. "When did you learn to shoot?"

"Dad started teaching me when I was eleven." I wrap my arms around his neck and bury my hands in his blond strands. He has the most beautiful hair I have ever seen. "Now you."

Sergei laughs and puts me down on the ground. He reaches for one of the guns I didn't recognize. While he's checking it, I walk around him to stand at his back. I wait until he lifts the weapon to take aim, then place my hands on his hips. Slowly I glide my hands along the waistband of his jeans to the front, then lower until my palms rest over his crotch.

"Angelina?" He looks over his shoulder at me. "What are you doing?"

"Didn't they train you to work under duress?" I smile and massage his dick through his jeans.

A corner of his mouth lifts. He looks back at the target and sends the bullet flying. It's a hit. I need to up my game. I press my breasts to his back, undo the jeans' button and lower his zipper. He shoots again. Another hit. Damn. I slide my hand inside.

"I don't think I've ever had sex in a field," I say and take out his cock, stroking it, enjoying the way it instantly gets hard. A shot rings out. I look up at the target. "Oh. Looks like you missed that one, baby. Am I distracting you?"

"No," comes his clipped answer.

"It's okay. It can happen to anyone." I duck under his raised arm and stand in front of him. Another shot rings out, but I don't turn to check to see where it landed. Instead, I drop to my knees and lick the tip of his cock.

Sergei groans.

"Don't mind me. Please proceed." I grip his now fully erect cock with my right hand, stroking him while my left hand slides under his shirt.

Whispered grumbling. Another shot, followed by a stream of Russian curses. I smile and lick his cock again. There is a thump in the grass next to me where Sergei throws his gun, and the next moment, I find myself lying on the ground with his body over mine.

"You little trickster." He bites at my chin while his hands are fumbling with my shorts. "Three misses out of five. Don't you dare tell anyone."

"Your secret is safe with me," I say, then gasp when his finger slides inside me.

He circles my clit with his thumb while his finger thrusts even deeper, and I feel my wetness spilling all over his hand. My back arches when he slides in another finger, stretching my walls, and I almost come, but the devil abruptly removes his hand.

"I have an amazing idea I'd like to discuss," he whispers next to my ear, then bites my earlobe.

"Now?" I snap and grab his cock. "The only discussion that's going to happen at this moment is between your dick and my pussy."

Sergei's arm wraps around my waist, and he rolls us until he's beneath me, with my body draped over his chest. I straddle him, positioning myself above his hard length, and slowly lower my body until I take him all in.

"How do you feel about getting a tattoo?" he asks and grabs my butt cheeks.

"Not happening," I breathe out as I ride him.

"It can be a small one." He squeezes my ass and lifts me up, holding me above his cock. "I'll teach you to shoot a sniper rifle in exchange."

His pale blue eyes watch me with a mischievous glint. I reach out and stroke his jawline with my finger. "And what would you like me to tattoo on myself, you maniac?"

Sergei's lips widen in a smile, and the next instant he slams me down onto his cock. I gasp, and bite my lower lip when he starts thrusting up into me.

"Nothing special," he says, quickening the tempo, "just a couple of words."

I throw my head back and enjoy the feel of him pounding into me from below. Sergei's hands slide under my shirt and rise to squeeze my breasts. I look down at him and run my hands up his corded arms, feeling his muscles bunch beneath my fingertips. "Which words?"

Sergei grins. My God, he is so beautiful. I hope I'll never see that vacant look in his eyes ever again. He slams into me again, and I scream as I come, but keep rocking my hips, riding the orgasm until I sag onto his chest. He moves his hands to my hips to hold me while he continues to thrust into me at a punishing pace. After a few more hard strokes he finds his release.

I cross my arms over his chest and place my chin on my hands, watching him. His eyes are closed, his breathing labored. He hasn't answered my question, but I adore the absolute bliss I see on his face.

"What words do you want me to tattoo, Sergei?"

He opens one eye. "Does it matter?"

"Of course, it matters." I scrunch my nose at him and shake my head.

"I was thinking something along the lines of *Prinadlezhit Sergeyu Belovu*." He closes his eye again. "On your lower back. What do you think?"

I gape at him, but once I'm over the shock, I blurt out, "You're not branding me as your possession."

"Why not?" He shrugs, then opens his eyes to look at me.

I stare at him. He's serious. A warm feeling explodes inside my chest, spreading until it fills my whole body. Pulling myself up so my head is right above his, I bend to whisper into his ear.

"Alright," I say.

Sergei growls, grabs me at the back of my neck, and claims my mouth.

CHAPTER
sixteen

I OPEN THE BAG OF DOG FOOD AND REACH FOR MIMI'S bowl as arms wrap around my waist, and a kiss lands at the top of my head.

"Why didn't you wake me?" Sergei asks and rests his chin on my shoulder, watching as I pour dog chow into the dish.

"You barely sleep as it is." I look at him sideways. "When are you planning to start sleeping in bed?"

It's been almost a month since we slept together for the first time. Every night since, we'd cuddle up together in bed, but when I wake up, Sergei would be dozing on the floor. I tried to convince him to stay with me, but he only shook his head, waited for me to fall asleep, then moved to his sleeping bag on the floor next to the bed.

"Is Felix around?" He always changes the subject when I start talking about this.

"I haven't seen him," I answer.

"He's probably at Marlene's. Let's go walk Mimi before breakfast."

Sergei whistles, and Mimi comes running around the corner. She lifts her head for Sergei to scratch her neck, then turns to me and licks my palm. I still find it hard to believe that such a scary-looking dog would have such a mild personality. Felix once said that Mimi can kill a man in under a minute, but looking at her as she runs around us, first nudging Sergei and then me with her nose, I wonder if he was just teasing me.

"I know what you and Felix did before you joined the Bratva," I say as we're walking down the sidewalk, making Sergei stop in his tracks.

"He told you?" he asks through his teeth. "When?"

"Some time ago." I don't mention that most of it I got from the pakhan, and Felix only filled in the gaps.

"I'm going to kill him."

I squeeze his hand. "How was it? The training, I mean. I know you can't talk about the missions."

Sergei takes a deep breath, wraps his arm around my middle, and leads us toward the park. "Believe it or not, I liked it," he says. "I wasn't in a good place when they brought me in, and they offered me purpose. A sense of belonging, in a way. It felt good. In the beginning, at least."

"How were the other guys in the group. Were you friends?"

"I can't say we were friends, exactly." He shrugs. "But we were in it together, so it created a sense of comradery."

"Do you know where they are now?"

"One died on a mission early on. David. He was a good kid. The other one, Ben, I killed," he says and looks down at me, waiting for my reaction. It was probably the guy Felix mentioned, the one who attacked him while Sergei was zoned out. I stare right into his eyes without blinking.

"And the others?" I ask.

Sergei watches me for a few seconds, then looks away and continues walking. "Kai and Az. Kai was an extremely deranged guy. Violent. Aggressive. When he got fixated on something, no one was able to get whatever it was out of his head. They had to restrain him a couple of times. Az was the complete opposite. Withdrawn. A recluse. Over all the years we spent together, I think he spoke less than twenty sentences to the rest of us." He smiles. "He played mean poker, though. Not even Felix, with all his cheating, could beat him."

"Az?" I ask. "That's an unusual name."

"It's a nickname. No one knew what his real name was. He wouldn't tell. Kruger, the guy who ran the unit, tried to beat it out of him. He collected him from the street with no documents, and when they ran Az's prints, they didn't get anything. But even when Kruger broke his arm, Az wouldn't say his name or anything. So, he ended up being just Az." He chuckles. "Crazy motherfucker."

"What happened to them?"

"I assume Kai is still working for the government. Az vanished six months before Felix and I left."

"Like lost on a mission?"

"Nope. Just disappeared." Sergei looks over at Mimi, who's running between some trees, and whistles. "There was a traffic accident. Az's wife was killed by a drunk driver. The following day, they found his house burned to ashes. No sign of Az."

"Jesus. Someone burned down his house?"

"He torched it himself."

"How can you be sure?"

"Everybody in the unit had a specialty. I was usually sent in when there was a need to clear a place of multiple hostiles. Az handled undercover missions, and when they needed someone dead without raising suspicion it was a hit. His favorite technique was burning things so thoroughly that the forensics team couldn't find shit."

"Do you think he's still alive?"

Sergei smiles. "Az is extremely hard to kill. He's alive."

We're just entering the house when Sergei's phone rings. The moment he looks at the screen and sees the number of the caller, his posture changes from relaxed to rigid. His arm comes around my waist, pressing me into his side as he lifts the phone to his ear.

"Diego," he says, and I stiffen. "What can I do for you?"

I can't hear Diego's reply, but from the way Sergei's arm around my middle relaxes, it's nothing bad. I exhale. For a moment, I was afraid he somehow found out where I am.

"Alright. Tonight, at ten. I'll send you the coordinates." Sergei cuts the call, "I'm meeting Diego's men tonight. Too bad he's not coming."

"He would never risk coming to the States personally," I say. "Do you think he knows I'm here?"

"I doubt it. He would have insinuated something if he did." He lowers his head and places a kiss on my cheek. "Don't worry, I'm ending that son of a bitch the moment an opportunity arises."

"Sergei, no." I grab his hand and turn him toward me. "He has too many allies. If you do anything to Diego, one of them will kill you."

"They can try." He smiles, but it's not a smile I'm accustomed to seeing on him. It's calculated and chilling. A smile of a predator who has his prey in his sights.

Every time I see Sergei in a suit, I'm amazed at the transformation. Gone is the scary-looking guy with disheveled hair and covered in ink. In his place, stands a businessman, someone who could pass as a company CEO or a politician.

I brush the nonexistent speck of dust from his jacket. "Where are you meeting Diego's men?"

"In one of the warehouses. Pasha won't let me use the clubs anymore."

"Why not?"

"I made a bit of a mess last time."

"What? You got drunk or something?"

He laughs. "I never drink, baby. I'm already crazy as it is."

"No." I press the tip of my finger over his lips. "You are not crazy. And I want you to stop saying that," I chide, and the corners of his lips lift like I've said something funny. "Wake me up when you come back, okay?"

"I won't be back before two or three. Diego's men like to talk."

"Doesn't matter." I rise up on my toes to lightly kiss his lips, but he wraps a hand around my back and presses me against his body, then attacks my mouth.

Behind me, Felix clears his throat. "Sergei. You'll be late," he says.

"Fuck you, Albert," Sergei mumbles into my mouth, then

resumes devouring my lips for five more minutes. He brushes my cheek with the back of his hand before he leaves.

"Were there more episodes?" Felix asks the moment Sergei closes the door behind him.

"No. Not during the past couple of weeks."

"Good." He walks toward the cupboard beside the fridge and pulls out his laptop. He carries it to the dining table and starts connecting cables.

"Do you plan on watching the meeting?"

"Yes." He nods. "There are two cameras in the north warehouse."

"Do you always do that?"

"Nope. But I have a bad feeling about this meeting."

"Why?"

"I don't know. I just do." He powers on the laptop. "Can you take Mimi out to do her business? I have to set up the connection."

"Sure."

The moment I take the leash off the wall hanger, Mimi rushes to my side and starts nudging my hand. I clasp the lead on her collar, knowing that it wouldn't do much if she decided to take off. She outweighs me by at least forty pounds. Good thing she's well-behaved, unless there are flowers around. I'll have to make sure to keep away from old Meggie's garden.

I initially planned on taking a short walk, but it's a beautiful night. Instead of staying close to home, I take Mimi toward a thicket of trees a few blocks away. We're almost to the edge when I notice a woman walking down the sidewalk and looking our way. She seems vaguely familiar, probably a neighbor we may have passed before. I lift my hand in a casual wave. The woman watches me for a second, looks at Mimi, then waves back and continues down the path.

I take a step toward the trees, but Mimi stays rooted to the spot, observing the surroundings, and letting out a strange low-key growl. She doesn't move, even when I pull on the leash, until the woman disappears around the corner.

"Not a fan of redheads, huh?" I mumble.

I spend almost an hour strolling around the neighborhood with Mimi. By the time I walk up the steps to the front door of Sergei's house, I'm ready to crash. The moment I open the door, however, Felix's raised voice wakes me up immediately. He's sitting at his laptop, talking with someone over the phone, but when he sees me, his head snaps up.

"Come here!" He motions with his hand and continues talking into the phone. "Try to approach him from behind and put the phone to his ear. Be careful, Yuri. He might not recognize you."

I rush into the kitchen and round the table so I am standing next to Felix. I open my mouth to ask what's going on, but when my eyes fall to the laptop screen, the words die on my lips. The video feed shows Sergei standing next to a man sprawled on the hood of a car. Sergei's right hand is around the man's throat as he bangs the guy's head against the vehicle. To the right of him, two more men are lying on the ground, neither of them moving. The one closest to Sergei has his head turned at an unnatural angle, while the other is face-down, with a pool of blood on either side of him. As I watch, a dark-haired man in a white shirt approaches Sergei from behind, holding a phone in his extended hand.

"Talk to him." Felix thrusts the phone into my hand.

I press the cell to my ear, but it takes me a few moments to collect myself enough to form the words.

"Sergei?" I choke out, not moving my eyes off the screen. He doesn't react. "Sergei!" I yell into the phone.

Sergei's head snaps to the side. He stares at the phone being held by Yuri for a heartbeat or two, then reaches out and presses it to his ear.

"Lisichka?" he asks, his voice perfectly calm, as if I caught him while he was drinking his morning coffee. "Is something wrong?"

I look at Felix, who nods and motions for me to continue. I just stare at him. What does he expect me to talk about?

"I . . . I was walking Mimi and she ate something. I didn't see what. She started coughing and then vomited."

Felix closes his eyes and nods.

"Maybe we should take her to the vet," I continue. "Can you come home?"

"Is she still vomiting?"

I look over at Mimi, who is sprawled over the sofa in the living room, snoring, then move my eyes back to the screen. Sergei still has his left hand wrapped around the guy's throat. "Yes. Can you please come?"

"I'll be there in half an hour." He lets go of the man and starts walking toward the other end of the warehouse where his car is parked. "Go get Albert so he can help until I get there, just in case. The old bat is probably asleep, wake him up."

He throws the phone to Yuri, gets into his car, and a few moments later leaves the warehouse. I lower the phone to the table and turn to Felix, who is slumped in his seat, shaking his head.

"What happened?" I ask and drop down onto the chair across from him.

"Diego Rivera sent his men to deliver the message that he'll be raising prices by twenty percent."

"Sergei went ballistic over that?"

"No. He just informed them that we won't be getting any more product from them." He sighs. "But when they told him Diego now holds a major market share after killing Manny Sandoval and taking his daughter, Sergei snapped."

"Jesus." I put my elbows on the table and press the heels of my palms to my eyes. "Does this happen often?"

"No. I think the mention of Rivera holding you triggered him. How much does he sleep?"

"I don't know. Four hours, maybe five." I shrug. "He usually goes to sleep after me, so I can't be sure."

"Do you two sleep in the same bed?"

"He waits until I'm asleep, then gets his sleeping bag and spends the night on the floor."

"Good. Keep it that way."

"I will most certainly not keep it that way," I say. "I've been trying to convince him to sleep in bed with me for weeks."

"What? Are you crazy?"

I cross my arms in front of me and pin Felix with my stare. "Did it ever occur to you that, maybe, if everyone stopped treating him like he's a wild animal, he may get better?"

"Did you see what happened there, Angelina?" He points to the laptop screen. "Do you know how much time he needed to overpower three armed men? Fifteen seconds!" he barks. "I think Roman and I made a mistake by putting all this on you. A girl as sheltered as you can't possibly understand what some people are capable of."

I tilt my head to the side and glare at him. "Do you know how they treat snitches in the cartel, Felix? Or thieves?"

"No."

"Then let me explain to you how very sheltered I've been." I lean back in my chair and look out the window at the garden. "There was this big tree not far from our house, just behind the flowerbed I loved playing around. I don't know what kind of tree it was, but it had very long and thick branches. Durable," I say. "When someone was caught giving intel to the authorities or other cartels, they would hang him from one of the lower branches. Hanging people was my father's favorite way of punishment. I was usually advised not to go to that part of the garden when the tree was occupied."

"Jesus fuck." Felix stares at me, his eyes wide. "They did that with children around? What if some of them saw the bodies?"

"Oh, we saw the bodies for sure. Everyone was present when someone was hanged. It was mandatory. A warning of sorts. My nana didn't want me to go there because of the smell."

"The smell?"

"Yeah, they sometimes left the bodies for a day or two. The stink was so strong, that even after they removed the corpses, the scent remained in my nose for days." I shrug. "Then, there was the hunt. That was used for thieves mostly."

I find it rather funny, the way Felix gapes at me, like he's seeing me for the first time. I'm pretty sure he knows what kind of hunt it was, but I continue anyway.

"My father's people would tie the thieves' hands behind

their backs and send them barefoot into the forest. A twenty-minute head start was what they usually got. Then, they would take the guns and go hunting. Sometimes, when there were multiple thieves being hunted, it would last the whole night. I would lie in my bed and listen to an occasional gunshot, wondering if it was a hit or miss." I put my palms onto the table and lean forward. "So don't you dare draw conclusions about what I can or can't deal with, Felix."

I get up and walk to the fridge, grab a can of Coke, then head into the living room to wait for Sergei.

"When Sergei comes, we'll pretend nothing happened," I say in passing.

"Angelina?"

I stop and look at Felix over my shoulder. "Yes?"

"Does this mean that you're staying?"

"Yes, it does."

CHAPTER
seventeen

·•·——— • ———📚Angelina📚——— • ———·•·

THE BLANKET STARTS SLIDING DOWN MY BODY. I GRAB the edge to keep it over me and just barely open one eye. It's still dark outside. There is another tug on the blanket, harder this time, and the cover slips from between my fingers.

"What time is it?" I mumble and bury my face in the pillow.

"Half past five," Sergei whispers in my ear and places a kiss on my nape. "I need your help with something."

"What?"

"This."

I feel his body pressing into my side, his hard cock nudging my hip, and smile. "We open at seven. If you want to be served, you'll need to wait."

"Oh, what a shame." His lips move to the side of my neck. "I'll have to help myself then."

I tilt my head and crack open my eyes, watching him as

he reaches for the drawer in the nightstand, and takes out the steak knife from my stash.

"I knew your obsession with sharp kitchen utensils would come in handy." He says, as cold metal presses to the small of my back where my T-shirt has ridden up. "I hope you're not too attached to this shirt, baby."

"What are you doing?"

"Helping myself," he says and, sliding the knife under my top, cuts the fabric all the way from my hem to the neck.

I start to turn around, but he presses his palm at the center of my back, keeping me in place. His other hand slides under my body and then glides down my stomach to between my legs.

"Sergei?"

"Shhh . . . You said you're not available at the moment," he says next to my ear and cups my pussy with his palm. "Therefore, you are not allowed to move. Or speak."

A shudder passes through my body at his words, and then another one when I feel the cold metal on my hip. One quick tug, and the band of my panties snaps. He shifts the knife to my other hip and cuts the band on that side. I reach down to remove the ruined panties, but Sergei's hand wraps around my wrist.

"I said . . . no moving, baby." He releases my hand and presses his palm on the base of my spine, keeping my pelvis pressed to the bed. "Not even an inch."

He lifts his other hand from my pussy, tracing his fingertips over my hipbone, then down my butt cheek, and between my legs. The panties which are still caught between my body and the bed start sliding away as he pulls them back and upward, the lacy material teasing my pussy. A small whimper leaves my lips from the unexpected sensation. Then, he changes the angle before drawing them out completely. I squeeze the pillow and bury my face into it, moaning.

"Not a sound, Angelina," Sergei whispers and thrusts his finger into me.

The pillow muffles my groan, but when he adds another finger, a small scream escapes me.

"Did I hear something, baby?" He strokes my spine with his palm while sliding his fingers deeper. "I think I did."

A second later, I feel his teeth on my butt cheek, biting. I moan loudly into the pillow from the pain he inflicts on me. He scissors his fingers inside my aching pussy and I feel the tell tale signs I am about to come. Sergei makes a 'come hither' motion with his fingers inside of me and my entire body combusts. I come all over his hand. Tremors are still rocking my body when Sergei's arm wraps around my waist, pulling me up until I'm positioned on the bed on all fours.

"Spread your legs, baby," he says and moves behind me. The arm around my middle tightens. "A bit more. Yes, that's perfect."

He removes his fingers from my pussy and slides his cock inside, slowly stretching my walls. I gasp. There is no better feeling in the world than that first slow thrust, when I can feel my body adjusting to him. When he's fully in, he wraps both of his arms around my waist and bends down to place a kiss in the center of my back. He's saying something in Russian, but I can't discern the words. A shiver rocks my body anyway. Slowly, he pulls out, then hammers into me again, and the pressure in my core intensifies. I grab at the pillow, squeezing it. Another thrust, stretching me even more as he buries himself to the hilt.

"Breathe, baby."

Yeah, I guess I forgot about that. I take a lungful of air as he continues to drive into me. With the punishing pace of his thrusts deep into me, I orgasm again. Blazing white stars explode in front of my eyes.

I expect him to keep going, but instead, he pulls out and wraps his arm around my middle, then eases me onto my back.

"I want you to look at me while I come inside you," he whispers and covers my body with his, entering me again.

I loop my legs around him and squeeze. "Why?"

His cock slides out then slams into me. "Because, when you look at me, I remember I'm still alive."

He starts rocking into me. Hard. Raw. Without leaving anything behind. Then faster, until I'm barely able to draw a breath between the thrusts. I come for the third time as he finishes in me.

Sergei

It's already morning. I should get up and start getting ready for work, but I can't make myself move.

"Albert has been searching for his carving fork for a week," I say as I stroke Angelina's back. "I saw it in the closet, behind your shirts."

"Can't he buy another?" she mumbles into my chest.

"Why? Did you get . . . attached to it for some reason?"

"Maybe." She moves up my body, nuzzling her nose into

the crook of my neck. "It has a really long handle. Amazing reach."

"So, you plan on keeping it?"

"Definitely. I took the santoku knife as well, since you offered. It's behind your collection of Stephen King books on the shelf."

How fitting.

"Why do you keep collecting weapons?" I ask. "Do you think someone here may wish you harm?"

"Of course not. It's a compulsion." She shrugs. "It makes me feel safer to know I have a weapon within close reach at any moment. I started doing that when I was seven years old, after I got kidnapped the first time."

My hand stills at the middle of her back. "The first time?"

"Yeah. I was fourteen the second time. They released me after my dad paid the ransom. After that, he sent me to the US."

"It must have been hard. Alone. In a new country."

"It wasn't that bad." She places her palm on my chest and sighs. "It was more strange than anything. But a good strange. Not having to watch over my shoulder all the time. People living ordinary lives."

"Did you have friends?"

"A few. But they were more like acquaintances. I found it really hard to connect with girls whose main preoccupations were what they were going to wear that day, or which boy noticed them." She snorts. "It seemed so silly. And I was a little jealous of them, I guess. I ended up preferring books to people."

"That reminds me. Albert asked me to tell you that a package arrived for you yesterday. He put it in the living room." I lower my head to whisper in her ear. "He said he looked inside and found a bunch of paperbacks with naked men on the covers, and now, he thinks you read porn."

"It's mental porn," she deadpans.

I burst out laughing. "Should I be concerned?"

"I don't know. Should you?" She tilts her head, slips her hand into my boxer briefs, and wraps her fingers around my cock. "Some of those books do set really high standards."

"You don't say?" I grab her around her waist and roll us until I'm lying on top of her. "You should know one thing, baby. I'm an extremely competitive person."

"Lucky me." She smiles and removes her panties.

CHAPTER eighteen

A TOUCH OF A HAND ON MY CHEST, AND MY EYES snap open. Angelina's breath brushes my side as she snuggles closer, and one of her legs comes over mine.

"Angelina?"

"Yeah?" she mumbles into my chest.

"You need to get back in bed, baby."

"No. Go back to sleep."

I close my eyes. She's been insisting on us sharing a bed for weeks, trying to sneak in the middle of the night to lie next to me. It's killing me to say no to her over and over again, but I can't risk it. She doesn't understand how fucking scared I am that I may hurt her in some way. So, like every night, I slide my hand down her body and remove her panties.

"It won't work this time, Sergei," she whispers and kisses my shoulder.

"What?"

"Your strategy of fucking me senseless, leaving me nearly comatose so you can put me in bed once I fall asleep."

"I'm such a scheming bastard." I wrap my arm around her waist and turn us so that I'm looming over her, then I lean in and kiss her.

"Yes, you are," she says and gasps when my finger starts teasing her clit.

I feather kisses on the side of her neck, biting when I reach the sensitive spot under her ear I found a few days earlier. Then, I move lower, until I reach her right breast. Angelina moans as I slowly lick around her nipple, keeping the same tempo as with my finger on her clit, before I switch to the other one. Her back arches as I trail my tongue down over her stomach until I reach her pussy. Two slow licks up her slit before I reach her clit and suck it into my mouth. The sounds she's making, like a little kitten, are driving me crazy.

She buries her hands in my hair, pulling as I lick her pussy a few more times before letting my tongue travel upward again, all the way to her lips.

"My little fox," I whisper into her mouth and take her face between my palms, gazing into her dark eyes. So fearless. And stubborn. Watching me without a trace of apprehension or reluctance in them. I wonder if she knows how madly in love with her I am. Kissing my way to the side of her neck, I nibble on her delicate skin. "You're the only thing that keeps my darkness away, lisichka." I kiss her shoulder. "If, one day, you decide you've had enough of my shit, just leave and never look back. And make sure you hide very well."

"Why?" she asks and wraps her legs around my waist.

"Because, I will follow and drag you back. And there's nowhere you'll be able to hide if I decide to chase you, Angelina."

She looks into my eyes as a mischievous smile forms on her lips. "Then, it's a good thing I'm staying."

I tunnel my fingers through her hair, tugging on the soft strands. Our gazes lock, and I thrust my cock inside of her. Without letting go of her, I slide out slowly before ramming back inside. My left hand wraps around Angelina's neck, feeling her heartbeat pulsing under my palm. I never realized how dead inside I've felt until this little fox stumbled onto my path and pulled me out of the abyss.

She pants as I pound into her, again and again, while she clutches at my shoulders. I'll probably have scratches all over my back tomorrow. That realization almost pushes me over the edge. My balls get tight, so I grit my teeth. Holding back, I change the tempo until I'm sliding in and out so slowly my dick feels like it's going to explode. Angelina lets out a tiny mewl, her muscles spasming around my cock, and I finally let myself come.

Angelina

Low whispered words wake me from my sleep, and for a moment, I think Sergei is talking on a phone to someone. But when I open my eyes, I find him lying on his back next to me, his eyes closed. He must have fallen asleep after we had sex earlier, forgetting to move me back up to the bed. Sergei's hand on my stomach twitches, and a Russian curse leaves his lips. He's having a nightmare again.

I know I probably should move away, as he told me to do when this happens, but if I just blindly obey, we'll never get past this. So instead, I lie on his chest and wrap my arms around his neck, placing my cheek next to his. His body stills for a second, then he starts tossing from left to right, trying to shake me off. I move my head to his shoulder and squeeze him harder.

"It's okay, big guy," I whisper into his ear, then place a kiss on his cheek. "It's okay."

His breathing is fast, labored, but he stops thrashing and turns his head to the side, our noses touching. I nudge the tip of his with mine and place a kiss on his tightly pressed lips.

His eyes are still closed, his mouth unmoving, but I keep kissing him. "I want you to take me for a ride on your bike again tomorrow." Another kiss. "Maybe you could let me drive for a bit, huh? I bet it's like riding a bicycle. Can't be that hard."

His breathing slows, but his hand on the small of my back is still shaking.

"I only tried riding a bicycle once, though, and ended up in a nettle bush on the side of the road," I continue babbling. "Nana Guadalupe was so mad when I got home covered in blisters and with bleeding cuts all over my legs."

Slowly, Sergei's eyes open and he blinks at me. "I would do anything for you, baby." He mumbles. "But, you're not touching my bike."

"Okay," I laugh, then place my cheek on his chest. "Let's go back to sleep."

CHAPTER

nineteen

"I LIKE THIS ONE." SERGEI POINTS AT THE RED leather jacket hanging on the mannequin.

I reach for the tag to look at the price and my eyes widen. "We can get this once I get access to my bank account."

"Roman said his guy would need at least two more weeks to have your new ID done. Good forgery requires time." He takes the jacket off the mannequin and offers it to me. "Try it on."

"It can wait. You've been buying everything for me. It doesn't feel right when I have loads of money sitting in my account."

"I like buying things for you." He dips his head and places a kiss on my lips. "Except for the bath stuff. There's so much different shit, I get anxiety every time I enter one of those fancy scented shops."

"Is that why you bought out the whole shop last time? I have enough shampoo to last me for two years."

Sergei takes a strand of my hair between his fingers, lifts it to his nose and inhales. "I like this one. We're buying more."

"Not until I go through at least half the stash I already have." I laugh.

"Okay." He lets my hair fall, then wraps an arm around my waist and pulls me against his body. "Let's pay for the jacket and go back home."

"Oh? Do you have something specific in mind?"

"Yes." His lips press to mine. "I told Albert we'll be busy the whole afternoon, and that I don't want to see him until tomorrow. He took Mimi with him."

"And what will we be busy with?"

His lips widen in a smug smile, and he leans to whisper in my ear. "I want to fuck you in every part of my home, on every piece of furniture. That way, when I zone out again, I'll have at least one of those spots in view. That will make it much easier to come back, don't you think?"

"I like that idea." I bite his lower lip. "I'm a big supporter of alternative therapy techniques."

He growls. "Cash register. Car. Kitchen. Let's go."

"I need to go to the bathroom after the cash register stop, but I have no complaints about the rest of the itinerary."

As soon as we're done paying for my jacket, Sergei ushers me to a mall restroom we find down one of the hallways, and sits on the bench out front to wait for me. I'm just washing my hands when the door behind me opens. I lift my head, glancing at the mirror, and spot the redheaded woman I saw while walking Mimi the other day. Our gazes meet in a reflection, and her lips widen in a smile.

"Angelina Sofia Sandoval," she says in an accented voice,

and cold dread rushes down my spine. "Someone would like to talk with you."

She takes a few steps toward me and places a phone on the counter next to the sink. I stare at the name shown on the screen, trying to control my erratic breathing, then pick up the cell and press it to my ear.

"Diego," I say, trying to make my voice sound calm. "What can I do for you?"

"Did you really think you could run away from me, you little bitch?" he barks.

"Yes. I hoped so."

He laughs like a madman. "I will enjoy breaking your spirit, palomita. No one gets away from Diego Rivera."

"I'm not going back to Mexico, Diego. Ever. As far as anyone is concerned, I'm a US citizen. So while I'm here, you can't do anything to me."

"I could kill you," he says. "Or even better, I could kill that Russian you've been fucking. Authorities won't blink if one of the Bratva's men ends up gutted on the street. Or with his car blown up. They'll probably thank me."

I suck in a breath and straighten my spine. "You won't dare kill him. It would mean the end of your collaboration with the Russians, and they're your biggest buyer."

"That's true. I would very much prefer to keep a good relationship with them, even if your crazy lover killed my men last time. Russians bring good money to the table, which means you're going to come back willingly," he sneers. "I've had people watching you for weeks, and from what they say, you seem very close to that demented Russian. Tell me, palomita, are you in love with Belov?"

"Of course not," I lie. "I'm just using him to get what I need."

"Then you wouldn't mind if one of my men waiting on the other side of the hallway shoots him on the spot?"

I grip the edge of the counter in front of me. "Please, don't."

A crazy laugh comes from the other side of the line. "The little runaway bitch has fallen in love. How convenient." He snorts, "So, what will it be? Are you coming back? Or am I killing your lover?"

"You won't touch Sergei." I close my eyes, trying to keep the tears from falling. "I'm coming back."

"Perfect. Now listen to me carefully. You'll text Juana the time you'll be alone in the house tomorrow and can slip out without anyone noticing. A car will be waiting for you."

"Tomorrow?" I choke out.

"Yes. You have one day to figure out how you'll explain the situation to your Russian. But keep one thing in mind. If he comes after you, he will be killed the instant he sets foot in Mexico. Do you understand?"

"Yes."

He laughs again. "I'm so looking forward to having you here, palomita. I'm getting quite bored with Maria lately, and I'm sure your pussy is much tighter than hers."

I throw the phone onto the counter and stare at my reflection. It's over. I swallow bile, turn toward the redheaded bitch, who's been standing by my side the whole time, and tell her my number. She saves it, nods, and leaves the bathroom with a smirk on her face. A few seconds later my phone pings with an incoming message. I look at the short text—Juana's number—and squeeze the phone with all my might.

One deep breath. Then another one. I turn on the water and splash some on my face. It helps a little, but I'm still close to breaking down. I splash more water, then look at my ghostly pale face, wondering what I'm going to do. Should I run? Diego will kill Sergei for sure in that case. I could tell Sergei the truth. He's more than capable of defending himself. But what if those scumbags set a bomb in his car? Or house? You can't defend yourself from a bomb.

No, there must be another way. Shit. Think, damn it. Police? Yeah, right.

Maybe I could go back to Mexico, then try to run again? It could work, but it would take me weeks or months until I convince Rivera that I'm docile enough for him to loosen the security. Doesn't matter. I will endure anything if it means being free of that son of a bitch. But it would also mean never seeing Sergei again.

I wrap my arms around myself, squishing the red leather jacket Sergei just bought for me in the process, and press my lips together to bottle up the scream that's been building inside of me since I saw Diego's name on that phone. No. I'm not falling apart here. Taking a deep breath, I will my legs to move.

I notice them the moment I leave the restroom. Two men in suits, standing at the other end of the hallway, their eyes fixed on Sergei. Diego wasn't lying.

"Everything okay?" Sergei asks when I approach him. "You look pale."

"Yup, all good." I nod and manage a fake smile. "I just have a headache."

He places his hand on the back of my neck and tilts my head up. "Do you want us to go to a doctor?"

"Of course not. It's just a headache. It'll pass. And anyway, we have plans, don't we?"

It takes immense control to keep my cool as he leans in and kisses me. Only the knowledge that Sergei could get killed if he finds out what's going on keeps me from bursting into tears. I take his hand and let him lead me out of the mall and toward his bike. All the while, I'm crumbling inside.

The ride back to Sergei's house lasts less than thirty minutes. I planned on using that time to think about how I'm going to slip out tomorrow, but instead, I spend the whole drive squeezing his waist, soaking in the feeling of having him close, and trying to save it in one of my mental vaults for safekeeping.

"Are you sure you're okay, baby?" Sergei asks when we get off the bike in front of his house.

I hang my helmet on the handlebar and turn toward him, noticing the way his pale hair reflects the light of the setting sun, the longer strands flowing in the breeze. Reaching out with my hand, I trace my finger along the line if his chin, and place my other hand at the center of his chest.

"I want you to make love to me so hard," I say, "that I forget everything else."

Sergei grabs me under my ass, lifts me up, and carries me toward the front door. I wrap my legs around his waist and take his face in my palms, placing kisses all over it. I start with his perfectly imperfect nose, then move to his forehead and eyebrows, sealing every single detail into memory.

"We'll start in the kitchen and move on from there," he says into my ear as he settles me onto the dining table. "I plan on covering the whole ground floor today."

"That's a lot of space." I smile and remove my jacket. "You sure you're up to it?"

My jeans and T-shirt are next, but when I take off my bra and reach for my panties, Sergei grabs my hand and moves it away. "We'll see." He smirks. "Lie down."

I lean back, pressing my back to the table's surface, and watch as he bends and places a kiss between my breasts. Slowly, he trails a line of kisses down my chest and stomach until he reaches my panties. He looks up at me with a smug smile, takes the waistband between his teeth, and pulls them down. When he has my panties removed, he takes my leg and places a kiss on my ankle, proceeds up along the inside of my thigh, then buries his face between my legs. I inhale sharply and grab his hair, panting as he licks at my clit—once, twice— and then sucks on it.

"I could spend the whole day just playing with your pussy," he murmurs and penetrates me with his tongue. He continues licking and sucking my pussy, squeezing my butt cheeks in the process, moving faster and faster until it feels like I'm going to explode. Then, he lightly bites at my clit, and my orgasm consumes me.

I am still panting when he places his hand at my nape and pulls me up to devour my lips. I taste myself on him—bitter- sweet. His other hand comes to my lower back to keep my body in place as he positions his cock at my entrance.

He pulls back to look me in the eyes. "I'm so in love with you," he whispers as he slides in me, bit by bit. I want to tell him the same, so much that it's tearing me apart from the in- side. Instead, I just press my lips together and clutch at his shoulders, not taking my eyes off him. I moan as he buries himself deeper in me, and I press my face into the crook of his neck. His hot breath fans at the skin of my shoulder, and I enjoy the feel of him sinking into me again and again. It's almost enough to make me forget about tomorrow. We come together in a mix of panting and groans.

"Couch, bedroom, or shower?" Sergei asks when he recovers his breathing.

"Shower," I mumble and wrap my legs tightly around his waist. There is no way I'm letting him out of my reach for a second longer than necessary.

"Okay." He chuckles and carries me up the stairs to his bathroom.

"I'm borrowing your shower gel today," I say as he sets me down under the water stream.

"I thought you like sugary scents."

I just shrug, grab a dark blue bottle off the shelf, squeeze a bit onto my palm, and start lathering my body.

Sergei comes inside the shower stall and, placing his finger under my chin, tilts my head up. "What's wrong?"

Water from the shower splashes at my side as I stare into his light eyes. "Nothing. Why?"

Dear God, even looking at him hurts because I know I'll be leaving tomorrow.

"You can't lie worth a damn, Angelina." He takes a step forward and leans in so we're face to face. "What is going on?"

"I have no idea what you're talking about."

Sergei puts his palms to the tiles on either side of my head and watches me with his lips pressed into a thin line.

I take a deep breath. "Are we going to finish this shower, or are you planning to keep looming above me like a gargoyle?"

"You don't get to lie to me. Ever," he says. "If you don't want to talk about something that's okay. If you need space, that's okay, too. I know that being with me can be overwhelming. But you won't lie to me. Deal?"

I look down and nod. "I don't want to talk about it."

"Alright. Do you need space?"

"No." I shake my head.

"If you want, I'll sleep in the other room tonight."

I still. No. This is our last night together, and I'll be damned if I let him sleep anywhere but in my arms. Placing my palm on his chest, I slowly slide it down until I reach his cock and wrap my hand around it.

"You're most definitely not sleeping in the other room," I say and squeeze his already hardening length.

Sergei sucks in a breath as he wraps his arm around my waist and presses me to his body. "This discussion isn't over, Angelina."

"We can continue tomorrow." I press a kiss onto the middle of his chest. "You promised me a sex tour of your place. I expect you to deliver. Or is it too much for you?" I look up, lifting an eyebrow.

A growling sound leaves his lips before he bends down and throws me over his shoulder. "The kitchen counter is our next stop," he says and taps my naked ass with his palm.

"Do you have plans for tomorrow?" I ask as I slide my hands up Sergei's back.

He's lying across the bed on his stomach, and I'm sitting on his lower back. It took me fifteen minutes, but I managed to convince him to let me massage him with one of my rose-scented oils.

"I have a meeting around noon," he mumbles into the pillow. "We can go for a ride afterward."

"Yeah," I choke out, then lean forward and press a kiss between his shoulder blades. "A ride sounds great, baby."

With every passing minute, I find it harder to pretend. It's like watching an hourglass with only a little bit of sand left in the upper bulb, and the grains fall faster and faster. I move my palms to Sergei's shoulders, then slide them down his arms—the very arms that carried the half-dead me out of that truck and saved my life. After I'm done with his arms I return to his back, my strokes becoming lighter, more of a ca- ress than a massage, until I feel his body relax and his breath- ing deepen. Sergei is a light sleeper, so I keep going for five more minutes before I carefully get down from the bed. I take my phone from the nightstand, send the message to the redheaded bitch saying that I will be ready to go tomorrow at noon, and head into the bathroom.

With that done, I lock the door, remove my clothes, turn on the water to scorching hot, and get inside the shower stall. The moment the spray hits me, I lean my back on the tiles. My entire body feels heavy with the weight of what I must do. My head droops forward first, then my legs give out, and I sink to the floor. I wrap my arms tightly around my knees and pull them close to my chest. I have nothing left to cling to, so this has to do. Maybe, if I squeeze tight enough, I'll be able to hold the shattering pieces of me together.

With the door locked, and the water drowning out all other sounds, I finally let myself break down. My tears, mixed with the shower stream, vanish down the drain.

What am I going to do tomorrow? I can't just disappear. No, I'll need to leave a note with an explanation. It'll be a bunch of lies, something that will convince Sergei that I decided to leave on my own accord and don't want to see him ever again. I will have to hurt him. And it'll have to be really bad if I want him to believe it. I can't risk Sergei chasing after me because Diego will have him killed. Of that, I'm one hundred percent sure. Maybe, one day, when I manage to escape from Diego, I can come back and look for him. Sergei will probably hate me by then.

I sit on the floor of the shower stall until the water runs cold, then put on that idiotic set of pajamas Sergei bought me and sneak under the bedcover next to him. It's already well after midnight, but I don't dare close my eyes and risk losing my final moments with him to sleep. I lie there and watch him until the light of the morning sun seeps into the room.

Sergei

"I shouldn't be long," I say while buttoning my shirt. "Two hours tops. We can eat something when I get back and then go for a ride."

Angelina's arms come around my waist. "Sounds good."

I turn around, and taking her face in my palms, I press a kiss onto her lips. "I bought you that junk food crap you like. It's in the cupboard next to the fridge."

"The ketchup-flavored chips?"

"Yeah. I don't know how you can eat that shit." I reach for my phone on the nightstand and head to the door. "Albert will be back with Mimi soon. Please remind him to feed her."

"Okay, baby." She nods and looks up at me. There's a strange look in her eyes, but it's gone in a blink.

I'm halfway to my car when I hear Angelina calling my name. I turn around to find her standing on the porch. She watches me for a moment, then runs down the steps and across the driveway. Instead of stopping when she reaches me, she jumps into my arms, wraps her legs around my waist, and crashes her mouth to mine.

"I'll miss you, Sergei," she whispers against my lips.

"Baby?" I mumble into her mouth. "I'm coming back in two hours."

"I know." She leans her head back and traces the tip of her finger down my nose. "Take care, big guy."

"I'm meeting with someone who supplies us with cars." I laugh. "He's almost eighty. I think I can take him on if he becomes hostile for some reason."

Angelina smiles, kisses me again, and wiggles her butt, so I put her down, squeezing her ass in the process.

"I'm going to get those chips now," she says and rushes back into the house.

As I watch her climb up the steps, a strange foreboding sensation settles in the pit of my stomach. It doesn't leave me even after I arrive at the meeting point. In fact, it only becomes stronger. Twenty minutes into the meeting, I decide to cut it short and head back home.

Half an hour later I'm parking the car on the driveway when Felix exits the house and stares at me with a grim face, his hands planted on his hips. I head to where he's standing on the porch while a sense of unease spreads through me.

"What's wrong?" I ask, climbing the steps.

"Angelina left."

"Alone?" I stop on the top stair. "Where did she go? I told her I'll be back in two hours. If she needed something, she could have waited."

Angelina likes going to the small grocery store down the street, but I prefer for her not to wander around alone.

"She left you a note on the bed. I saw it when I went to look for you two," Felix says and looks away. "She's not coming back, Sergei."

I stare at Felix, processing what he just said, then rush inside the house. I take three stairs at a time and run to my bedroom. There, on a tidily made bed, lies a lonely piece of paper. For a few moments, I just look at it as panic unfurls inside me. I take a deep breath, approach the bed, and read the neatly handwritten note.

Sergei,

For quite some time, I've been thinking about my life and everything that has happened. I've decided I need a fresh start. I contacted one of my father's friends earlier this week, and he arranged for me to get an ID so I can access my money and leave the States. While I truly enjoyed spending time with you, I realize that if I want to bring order into my life, I need to cut connections with everything that ties me to my past.

We had some nice moments together, but sometimes you scare the shit out of me, and I think it's time we part ways. I thought I could deal with your issues, but the truth is, it's too much, and it's best that I leave. I booked a one-way flight to Europe, and I don't plan on coming back.

Thank you for everything and take care.
Angelina.

I stare at the paper in my hand, then crumple and throw it across the room. Rage, stronger than any I've ever felt, consumes me. Felix's voice reaches me from behind, but it gets weaker with every passing second until all I can hear is the ringing in my ears, and then nothing.

Angelina

They're late. I turn around and look up and down the street, wondering if, by some stroke of luck, Diego changed his mind. Even though it's rather warm, I keep the red leather jacket on. Other than a few toiletries and a change of clothes, it's the only thing I took with me when I sneaked away from Sergei's home. I planned on leaving the jacket as well—it was crazy expensive—but I couldn't make myself do it.

There's also one of his small knives hidden at the bottom of my backpack. There is no way I'm going to Diego unarmed. A gun would have been a much better option, but it was harder to hide.

I wrap my arms around my waist and debate if I should call the redheaded bitch, Juana, to ask what's going on when I notice a black car approaching. A sensation of falling overtakes me. It looks like I'm not that lucky after all. The car stops in front of me, and a short man sitting in the driver's seat lowers the window. He's in his late forties and an American. The car itself is maybe ten years old and is well used. Nothing even remotely is suspicious about it. Apparently, Diego doesn't want to risk the boarder authorities looking too closely at the passengers.

"Do you have my documents?" I ask.

"Yes."

I take a deep breath, throw the phone Sergei bought for me into the bushes, and walk around the car to get into the passenger side door. "Let's go then."

Sergei

"Sergei?" Roman's voice reaches me from somewhere on my right.

I open my eyes and, for a couple of seconds, I can't grasp where I am until I notice familiar details. The bookshelves to the left are still in place, probably because they're anchored to the wall. They are the only things, other than the bed where I'm sitting, that are still intact. The two recliners lie overturned near the opposite wall from where they should be, some of their parts are missing. The dresser, with clothes spilling out of it, is askew atop one of the chairs. Pieces of wood, fabric, and books are scattered all over the room, making it look like an earthquake or a tornado has hit it.

"Sergei? Are you with us?"

I look up.

Roman is standing in the doorway with Felix lurking behind him. Mimi, with her head on her paws and eyes peering at me, is lying on the floor in front of them.

"How long?" I ask.

"Four hours." Roman takes a few steps but stops when he reaches the middle of the room. "Felix called me the moment you started trashing stuff, but when I arrived, you were already done with this floor."

"Shit." I shake my head. "How does the downstairs look?"

Roman scans the room around him and shrugs. "Pretty much the same. Good thing Felix thought to lock the armory before you reached it."

Thank God for that. I don't remember anything after reading Angelina's note. Closing my eyes, I take a deep breath. I need to get out of here.

"Albert, where are the keys to my bike?" I ask as I get up from the bed.

"You're staying put," Roman snaps and points his cane at me. "Sit back down."

"Roman, don't," Felix mumbles from behind him.

"I'm not letting him go anywhere in this state. He'll either crash or kill someone."

I tilt my head and look at my brother. We're pretty evenly matched when it comes to strength, and I would love nothing more than to work off some of the frustration and rage that's boiling inside of me with a good fight. But Roman can't take me on, not anymore at least, his knee is too fucked up. And if I lose it during the fight, I may go for a kill. I don't want to annihilate my brother, no matter how annoying he might be.

"Back off, Roman." I head for the door, but as I pass him, his hand shoots out and wraps around my neck.

"She isn't worth it, Sergei."

I grab his shirt and lean forward, staring him down. "Don't you dare say a word about her," I bite out. I won't let anyone talk badly about Angelina. Even though it kills me to admit it, she made the right decision to save herself. No one should be burdened with someone as fucked up as me. "Not a word. You hear me, Roman?"

We stare at each other for a few moments, then Roman shakes his head and removes his hand from my neck. "Please, don't get yourself killed."

I let go of his shirt and walk to the doorway, but then stop. "You promised Angelina you would ask about her nana. Do you have any intel?"

"Not yet. My contact in Mexico called this morning and said he'll be able to check the Sandoval compound this weekend. It sounded like Diego is throwing a party."

"Good. Let me know the moment he calls."

"Why?"

"I plan on getting Angelina's nana out of there if she's alive."

"Damn it, Sergei! You're not going to Mexico!"

I ignore his yelling and step out of the room. "You may want to call Mendoza and see if he can double the quantity next month," I throw over my shoulder. "Or find another supplier because I'll be killing Diego while I'm down there."

Chapter Twenty

Angelina

T HE BIG IRON GATE SLOWLY SWINGS TO THE SIDE, ITS hinges squeaking in the process. Every time I came home, I told my dad the damn thing needed to be replaced. He always said he was going to do it, assuring me that when I returned the next time, a new gate would be waiting for me. Now, it just reminds me of my father and how Diego slaughtered him.

I squeeze my hands into fists and regard the surroundings as the car heads toward the massive one-story mansion at the end of the road. Every second that passes, dread keeps building in my stomach. I thought I would never again see this place, or at least I hoped I wouldn't. It's strange. I never thought I could both love and hate a place as I do my childhood home.

The driver parks the car beside the wide, stone steps leading to the ornate front door. Two men, rifles strapped over their backs, stand guard on either side of it. Nothing has changed. Taking my backpack, I exit the car and climb up the steps, trying my best to keep my face expressionless.

I don't plan on advertising how utterly terrified I am. People say that fear of the unknown is the strongest. Well, they don't know shit, because I know exactly what's waiting for me here, and I would trade anything for ignorance. Just before I reach the threshold, the door opens. Nana Guadalupe rushes out and sweeps me into her arms.

"*Mi niña*." She sniffs. "Why the hell did you come back here? When Diego told me, I didn't believe him."

"Long story, Nana," I whisper into her hair and squeeze her frail body to mine. Seeing her safe and well makes this all a little bit easier. "I was so afraid that Diego hurt you."

She leans back and takes my face into her palms. "What were you thinking Angelina?" She shakes her head. "You should have stayed in the US."

I open my mouth to reply but a burst of male laughter that comes from the other side of the hall makes me falter.

"Well, if it isn't our little runaway?" Diego shouts, and my heartbeat quickens. I look up to see him wobbling toward us. He is even more disgusting than I remembered— oily hair, and a stained T-shirt stretched over his enormous belly.

"Diego." I nod and walk around Nana to stand in front of her, hiding her with my body. I'm still afraid he might hurt her.

"I hope you enjoyed your little trip, because you won't be leaving the compound ever again." He comes to stand before me, his lips stretching into an evil smile. "Welcome home, palomita." He backhands me so hard that I crumple to the floor.

There is something wet at the side of my face. For a moment, I think it must be Mimi licking my cheek. I open my eyes and turn my head only to wince when pain shoots through the left side.

"Drink this." Nana Guadalupe thrusts a pill in my mouth and presses a glass to my lips. I swallow the painkiller and gulp down some water, trying to move my jaw as little as possible.

"What happened?" I choke out.

"The bastard hit you. You blacked out. I had one of the boys bring you here."

I sit up in bed and look around my old room. In a way, it feels like I never left.

"Do you know what Diego is planning for me?"

"He's throwing a party tomorrow evening," she says. "He's going to announce that the two of you are getting married."

"When?"

"Wednesday." She takes my hand and squeezes my fingers. "Why Angelinita? Why come back when you knew what was going to happen?"

I look up at her, feeling the tears gather at the corners of my eyes. Then, I tell her everything. By the time I finish, I'm crying so hard I can barely see her face through all the tears.

"Are you in love with your Russian?"

"Yes," I whisper and cover my mouth with my hand. It's hard to speak about Sergei.

"Give me his number, I'll try calling him. He must come to get you out of here."

"No. Diego will just kill him."

"Angelina . . ."

"No, Nana. What's done is done. I won't risk him dying because of me."

The door to my room opens and Maria enters, a small smile stretching her lips. "Diego is waiting for you in his bedroom," she says and her smile widens. "Don't let him get restless."

She turns and closes the door behind her while panic and terror grip my insides.

"Where is my backpack?" I whisper.

Nana takes it from the table and passes it to me with a look of horror written all over her face. She knows very well what's next. I take the backpack and thrust my hand inside, rummaging through its contents until my fingers wrap around the sleek blade of Sergei's throwing knife. I pull it out.

"You can't kill Diego with that."

"I know," I say, get up off the bed, and head into the bathroom.

Placing the knife on the counter next to the sink, I remove my jeans and panties, then start rolling up my left sleeve.

"What are you doing?" Nana Guadalupe asks from the doorway.

"I heard Diego say he doesn't want to fuck whores when they have their period," I say and reach for the knife. "He said he finds it disgusting."

I place the tip of the blade on my left upper arm. Gritting my teeth, I press it lightly until it pierces the skin. I hear Nana gasp when blood starts seeping from the small cut. Reaching for the panties on the counter, I press the beige fabric onto the wound, making sure to smear the blood so it looks as genuine as possible. When there is enough blood on my panties,

I put them on again, and grab a towel from the rack, pressing it hard against the incision.

"Find me something to wrap around my arm," I say and start opening the cupboards, hoping to find a first aid kit. The cut is not that big, it should stop bleeding soon enough, but it would be safer if I put something over it to hold the skin together. There's no medical kit, but I still have a little luck left, because I find a box with Band-Aids.

Nana Guadalupe rushes back into the bathroom. She's holding a pillowcase and tears a wide ribbon from it. When she's done, she places two Band-Aids over the cut and wraps the cotton strip around my arm.

"Put another one over it," I say. My shirt sleeves are wide, so the makeshift bandage shouldn't be visible underneath. I can't risk the blood leaking through. Diego might notice it.

After she wraps another swath of fabric around my arm, I roll the sleeve down, put on my jeans, and head toward the door.

"You think this will stop him?" Nana asks from the bathroom doorway.

"It won't stop him from raping me eventually," I say, "but I hope it will buy me a few days at least."

The asshole took my father's bedroom.

I stare at the big white door at the end of the hallway for a long time before taking a deep breath and twisting the knob to go inside.

Diego is sprawled on the bed, fully naked, holding his small dick in his meaty hand, stroking it. When he sees me, he motions for me to approach. I head toward the bed, swallowing the bile. Just looking at him makes me sick.

"I was so looking forward to this, palomita." He smiles. "Take off your clothes and come here. I've been preparing myself for you."

I stop at the edge of the bed and start unbuttoning my jeans, praying to all that is holy that I was right, and he won't want to have anything to do with me when he sees the blood. Funny how such a repulsive, dirty man can find a woman unclean if she has her period. I undo my jeans and slide them down, watching his face while holding my breath.

"You filthy bitch!" he yells, his eyes glued to my panties then springs up, gripping me by the forearm. "Did you do it on purpose? Did you mess with your period?"

I look down, pretending surprise. "I didn't notice it. It probably just started."

He stares into my eyes, releases my arm, and slaps me across the face. "Pull your pants up."

I yank my jeans up and turn to leave, but his hand shoots out, grabbing my wrist. "Where do you think you're going? Your mouth isn't soiled." He grins and sits down on the edge of the bed, widens his legs, and tugs at my arm. "Kneel."

I look down at his pitiful cock and then up until our gazes meet. He will probably kill me if I decline. My death will break my nana's heart, but I will not kneel and suck the dick of the man who killed my father. Even if it means death.

Lowering my head until our eyes are barely inches apart, I smile, and then spit into his face. "Suck your own dick, Diego."

He roars, throws me onto the bed, and climbs over me, wrapping his hands around my neck and squeezing. I gasp and claw at him, trying to remove his fingers as my lungs scream for air. I'm failing. My vision starts dimming and dark spots form in front of my eyes, but I keep thrashing, trying to get him off me. I should have brought Sergei's knife with me. I'm halfway unconscious when the hands lift from around my neck, and I gulp in air, coughing. Another slap lands on my face, then one more.

"I can't wait for Wednesday," Diego sneers above me. "Filthy or not, I'm going to fuck you in front of everyone, palomita. Nobody says no to Rivera!"

He hits me again, then pushes me off the bed. I barely manage to get my hands up in front of me to break the fall.

"I want you dolled up for the party tomorrow. Make sure you cover the bruises well. I don't want people to think I'm not treating you like you deserve." He laughs.

I suck in a breath, slowly get up from the floor, and turn to face the bastard while he leans back in the bed with a big smile on his face.

"Fuck you," I rasp, swipe the back of my hand over my mouth to wipe away the blood, and head for the door.

Diego's insane laughter follows me.

Sergei

Distant voices reach me, but I don't register the words at first. Everything sounds like muffled mumbling. Gradually, they become stronger and coherent. When my vision clears, Felix is standing on the other side of the living room, with Roman and the doctor on either side of him.

"Sergei?" Felix takes a step toward me.

"What?"

"He's back." He sighs and turns to the other two men. "You should go. I'll call you."

I wait for Roman and the doc to leave, then get up from the floor, wincing at the pinpricks sensation along my legs. "What happened?"

The last thing I remember is coming home after spending two days riding around the city, only stopping to get gas, or when I needed to eat and could no longer ignore my body's demands. And then nothing. "I found you here when I came by at noon. You've been staring at the wall for hours."

"What time is it?"

"Seven in the evening."

Well, that explains why my legs feel like they're made of lead. "What was Roman doing here?"

"He came to talk with you. Brought Doc with him in case you didn't come out of it."

"What did he want to talk about?"

"His Mexico contact called," he says and follows me into the kitchen as I walk to the fridge to take out a bottle of water. "He found Guadalupe Perez. She's still at the compound."

"Good. See if you can get her an ID that would work for the routine border crossing. It shouldn't take long. I'll go get her as soon as you have it."

"Okay." He nods but keeps looking at me in a strange way.

I've known Felix for fifteen years, and recognize most of his tells. "What is it?"

"Did Angelina act out of character before she left?"

I grip the edge of the counter and stare at the white tiles in front of me, gritting my teeth. It's hard thinking about her. "Maybe a little. When I thought about it, I figured it was probably because she was already planning on leaving."

"Did someone approach her?"

I swivel around to face him. "No. Why?"

"Because she's not in Europe. She's in Mexico, Sergei. With Diego Rivera."

"What?!" I slam the glass I'm holding onto the counter, and it shatters into smithereens, pieces of glass flying everywhere.

"Roman's contact said he saw her today, at the lunch party Diego organized. Rivera announced that the two of them will be getting married on Wednesday."

I close my eyes and take a deep breath, trying to go over the past week in my mind. Angelina was acting strange the morning when she disappeared, so something must have happened prior. The mall. She spent too much time in that restroom.

"I need you to access the inside cameras of the mall where we went the day before she left," I say.

"Sure. I'll get my laptop."

I stare at the black-and-white photo of a woman Felix pulled out of the police records. Then, I move my eyes to the right, where the still shot from the camera feed shows the same woman exiting the mall restroom just a few minutes before Angelina came out.

"Juana Ortiz," Felix says. "There is no proof, but the

note in the report says she's suspected of working for Diego Rivera."

"They probably threatened Angelina with killing her nana. Why didn't she say anything, damn it?"

"I don't think they threatened her nana, Sergei. Look." He brings up another angle of the recording. Another end of the same hallway. Juana walks toward two men standing by a vending machine, nods, and they leave.

"I checked the other cameras, as well," Felix says as he brings up the video of Juana leaving the restroom again. "They were standing fifty or so feet directly behind you. The taller one was concealing a gun under his jacket. It can be seen from another camera. Pay attention to where Angelina looks right after she exits."

He plays the video and zooms in on the door to the restroom. The camera was probably mounted close by, because when Angelina walks out, I can clearly see the terrified expression on her face as she looks up and over my shoulder, straight in the direction where the men were standing. Her eyes wander to me, then back to the goons for a moment before she heads my way.

"I think they threatened to kill *you*," Felix says.

I stare at the paused recording, my eyes glued to Angelina's frightened face, and smile. "I'm going to slaughter them all."

I put the last of the guns into the hidden compartment in the floor of my car, close the trunk, and whistle for Mimi, who dashes down the steps and jumps onto the back seat.

I get behind the wheel and close the door. I'm just reaching for the ignition when the passenger door opens and Felix gets in.

"Where do you think you're going?" I ask.

"To Mexico." He throws his backpack onto the back seat next to Mimi and reaches for the seatbelt.

"You're not going." I lean over him and open his door. "Out."

"No."

"This is not a fucking geriatric excursion. I'm infiltrating a cartel compound that's guarded by at least thirty armed men."

"Exactly," he snaps. "You need backup. And a driver in case you get shot and can't drive back."

"You're too old for this shit. I am not letting you risk your life for me, Albert. Out."

"Would you fucking stop with your 'I'm invincible crap'? Do you have a death wish? Is that it? Because we both know that if you go in without surveillance backup, the chances of you getting out alive are zero!"

"I've completed missions with more hostiles several times."

"Yes, but then you only had yourself to worry about. How do you plan on leaving that place with two women in tow? They'll slow you down. Not to mention the small army that'll be chasing you."

"I'll manage."

"You'll die!" he yells into my face, then switches his gaze to the windshield. "I'm coming."

Mimi barks from the back seat.

"See? That's two against one."

I watch him as he arranges the collar of his shirt, moves his glasses up his nose with his finger, and leans back in his seat.

"Fucking perfect," I mumble and start the car.

Felix is silent for the first five minutes or so, then starts complaining about Marlene. I tune him out. I'm not in the mood to offer relationship advice at the moment.

"What happened in Colombia, Sergei?" he asks suddenly.

I light a cigarette and give him a sideways look. "That again?"

"Yes." He turns toward the window and stares out. "Please."

I sigh. "That politician Kruger sent me to terminate. He was into human trafficking."

"I know. That much was in the mission file."

"I offed him while he was having breakfast in his garden. Everybody knew he had girls for sale and kept them somewhere in the compound. I planned on infiltrating it, to look for them. Kruger said no. He assured me the police would find them and get them free when they came to investigate." I lean back in my seat and take a drag of the cigarette. "Police came. Then left. They didn't bring anyone out, just sealed the place up and were gone."

"So, they didn't find the girls?"

"Oh, they found them," I say.

"I don't understand."

"I went in after the police had left. Took me a while to find the door to the basement." I shut my eyes for a second, trying to suppress the images of bodies scattered around. "They were already dead. Every one of them shot in the head. Colombian police were obviously involved in the trafficking.

They disposed of the girls when they found them, so the girls wouldn't be able to talk."

"Jesus."

"I'm not certain, because they were all dirty and just skin and bones, but I don't think any of them were older than sixteen." I turn to look at Felix. "Ten kids died because of me. If I had gone in before the police, they would be alive today."

"It's not your fault," he barks. "You were following strict orders."

"I did." I nod and light another cigarette. "Like Kruger's perfect little killing machine is supposed to."

Felix looks away. The rest of the drive passes in complete silence.

We manage to cross the border without any trouble. When we get off the highway onto a side road that leads to the Sandoval compound, I check the map. I've marked all the spots where Sandoval's men usually kept guard. I doubt that Diego bothered to change the locations. I take another side road that should get us almost to the compound with only one checkpoint along the way. When we near the guards' location, I park the car behind some foliage and get out to change and arm up.

"What the fuck is that?" Felix mumbles behind me as I'm taking out the weapons.

"Crossbow." I open the box with bolts and start counting them. "It's a new model Luca gave me last month to try out."

"You're deranged." He tsks. "Can't you do anything the normal way? Why not dispatch them with a knife?"

"Because there are usually at least three men at this checkpoint. And it's not dark enough for sneaking up on that many targets."

"So, you picked a fucking crossbow? Who do you think you are—damn Van Helsing?"

"Oh, shut up already."

"What about a sniper rifle?"

"Not on this terrain. I'd need to get too close for that." I strap a knife to my thigh and take the crossbow. "I'll be back in an hour. Prepare the cameras, and I'll set them up around the compound as soon as it gets dark."

"How many?"

"Twelve. Have Mimi do her business, but don't wander around. No one should find us here, but have a gun at ready, just in case."

"You really think you can pull this off? It's at least thirty security guards, Sergei. Plus, the guests, who will probably all be armed."

"It's nothing a bit of C-4 can't handle," I say and head in the direction of the guards.

"We drove all the way here with C-4 in a trunk?" he whisper-yells after me. "How much did you pack?"

I look over my shoulder and wink at him. "All of it, Albert."

There are four of Diego's men around the cabin they use as a checkpoint. One is standing by the vehicles parked off to the side, while the rest are sitting on the porch, eating. I don't like killing people when they are in the middle of a meal—seems disrespectful—but I'm on a really tight schedule here.

I aim the crossbow at the lone man, and when I'm sure no one is looking in his direction, I let the bolt fly. It impales the side of his head, but I miscalculated the angle. Instead of a straight drop, the impact propels the guy onto the hood of the car before his body rolls to the ground. The heads of the other men snap in the direction of the vehicles, but they can't see what happened from where they are.

I load another bolt into the crossbow and wait.

Two guys take their guns and head around the cabin toward the cars, calling for their friend. The moment they round the corner, I shoot the guy who remained on the porch. I leave the crossbow on the ground and, taking out the knife, run to the vehicles from the other side.

If they see the body, they may call the base to report it, and I can't have that. The main advantage of my plan for tomorrow is the surprise factor. If I don't have that, everything may go to hell. Using my gun is not an option because we're too close to the compound and someone may hear it. Going against two armed men only with a knife is not the wisest course of action, but it'll have to do. I plaster my back to the side of an all-terrain truck, right next to the dead guy, and wait.

One of the men turns to look back toward the cabin, and I use that moment to jump in front of the other guy and slice his neck. The moment his body hits the ground, I bury the knife in the other man's side and grab his gun with my free hand. Two more stabs and he's done.

I hide the body of the first guy I offed in one of the trunks. It takes me fifteen minutes to drag the other three to the cars and hide them, too, before I'm ready to head back. It's time to set the stage for tomorrow.

Angelina

"Let me see." Nana Guadalupe takes my chin between her fingers and tilts my face to the side, inspecting the bruises that are now a disgusting shade of purple.

"Nana, I want you to get me a gun," I say and turn to face her. "It has to be today. I don't know when the makeup artist and hair stylist are scheduled to arrive tomorrow morning."

"And what do you plan to do with the gun, Angelinita?"

"I'm killing Diego tomorrow."

"No!" She grabs my hand. "Even if you manage to shoot him, his men will kill you on the spot."

"He told me he plans on fucking me in front of everyone after the wedding," I say and squeeze her hand. "If he tries, I'll need that gun, Nana. Because I'm not letting that son of a bitch rape me on the dining table in front of his guests."

I've been thinking about my options and came up with nothing else. If I try to run, there are three possible outcomes. One, I fail, and Diego kills me right away. Two, I fail, Diego catches me, and drags me back. And three, I manage to run away, and he kills Sergei. The first two are basically the same, because if he drags me back, I'm as good as dead. He'll just torture me for defying him before he kills me. The third is out of the question because I am absolutely sure he will kill Sergei to punish me for making him a laughingstock of the compound by running away from him twice.

I take my nana's face between my palms and look into her warm eyes. "Will you get that gun for me?"

She presses her lips together and nods.

───────◆──❦── Angelina ──❦──◆───────

I SIT ON A CHAIR IN THE MIDDLE OF THE ROOM AS TWO girls fuss with my hair and look down at the white silk dress I'm wearing. Knowing it was Diego who chose it, it's not that bad. I expected a small piece of material that would barely cover my ass and breasts, but the dress is rather modest, with a high neckline and a skirt that flares from the waist. It's sleeveless, so I had to cover the cut on my upper arm with foundation. I strapped the gun Nana got me around my right thigh with the elastic band that I extracted from the waistline of my sweatpants. It's not the best solution, but it works. Thank God the skirt is wide, so the gun is well concealed under the heavy silk material. If Diego had chosen something short or tight, it would have been impossible to hide it from view.

The door behind me opens and Maria walks inside wearing a short red dress with sequins. There's a fake smile plastered all over her face, and her eyes are watching me with malice.

"You will be late. Diego won't be pleased," she says.

I still can't understand how she can let that pig fuck her every night. Just looking at him makes me want to puke.

"From what I hear, he's in a good mood," I comment.

The drinking and singing started hours ago. I can hear the laughter and yelling from here, even though my room is on the opposite side of the house.

"You should add more makeup over the bruises, Angelina. The bluish hue is still noticeable."

"You, too," I say and watch her turn toward the mirror, inspecting her face. So, he hits her, as well. Looks like I'm not that special after all. "Leave. I'm coming down in a minute."

After Maria leaves, I send away the makeup girls. When I'm finally alone, I sit down on the bed and close my eyes, letting my mind drift to that last evening with Sergei. I can't believe he let me rub the rose oil all over him. He still smelled faintly floral when he went to the meeting the following morning. My lips widen in a smile at the recollection, but a single tear slides down my cheek. God, I miss him so much. I wish we had more time together.

Another round of rowdy laughter reaches me, bringing me back to reality. Reaching up with my hand, I brush away the stray tear, then place my hand on my thigh to feel the gun hidden under the silky material. Time to go. I get up and leave the room.

"Palomita!" Diego roars from his spot at the head of the table that has been set up the garden. "Come here."

I squeeze my hands into fists and walk across the wide

patch of grass until I reach the cobbled patio where everyone has gathered. There are around forty people, mostly men. Some of them I know because they were my father's associates and business partners who came to our house quite often. Based on the way they avoid looking at me, they probably know I'm not here voluntarily, but none of them will stand up for me. Business always comes first—morals be damned. The rest watch me pass, spewing dirty jokes, laughing like pigs, and congratulating Diego on his choice.

As I near the head of the table, I notice the priest sitting on Diego's left, and, for a fleeting second, hope rises in me. I know him. My father regularly donated money for homeless kids his church takes care of. However, when he looks up at me, there's a look of terror in his eyes, as well as a warning as he cuts a sideways glance at Diego. Hope fades as realization sets in. Father Pedro has been threatened, too. I wonder if my disgusting soon-to-be husband will force the priest to stay and watch when he tries to rape me in front of everyone.

"Isn't she beautiful?" Diego asks as he grabs my wrist and pulls me down onto the chair.

I feel his meaty hand reach for my leg, just above my knee, and go utterly still. If he moves his palm just a few inches up my thigh, he'll feel the gun I have strapped there.

"Not as plump as I like them, but she'll do." Diego laughs, and I exhale when he removes his hand to reach for a wineglass.

He's already wasted, as is everyone else around the table. The priest will probably have to marry us while we're seated, because I doubt Diego will be able to stand. I look over at the house and see Nana Guadalupe standing there with her right hand hidden inside her knitted cardigan. She's staring at me, but then her eyes shift to Diego. Why is she wearing that thing? It's scorching hot, and I'm already melting in my dress. She looks back at me, then down at the watch on her left wrist, and smiles before heading in our direction. I watch her through narrowed eyes as she walks around the table and stands behind my chair.

"Stay down," she whispers into my ear, grabs the back of my chair, and pushes it sideways with me still on it. As I topple over, a whooshing sound pierces the air.

I land on my shoulder and yelp, but my cry gets lost in the epic boom that reverberates somewhere near the guard gate. There are a few moments of utter silence, and then three more explosions—one after the other. People start yelling, jumping from their chairs, and reaching for their weapons. I roll until I am under the table and look up to see Nana Guadalupe crouching next to me, clutching a gun in her hand. She's still smiling.

"What's going on?" I yell as I pull my skirt up and take out my weapon, but I don't think she hears me because the explosions continue all around us, each less than a few seconds apart. It sounds like the end of the damn world. I peek around the tablecloth to check out what's going on just in time to see the auxiliary building where we store vehicles collapse. The guests and security guards run across the lawn with their weapons raised, all looking confused, and I notice one of the men fall to the ground. For a moment, I think he must have tripped, but then my eyes find a big red dot in the center of his forehead.

In the brief interlude between explosions, I hear another whooshing sound, and see another man drop.

"It's a sniper!" someone shouts, and people start running for cover.

Two security guards turn toward the house only to end up on the ground soon after. The guests run in a wild stampede to their parked vehicles, and one by one, the cars race toward the open gate that's now hanging off its supports, destroyed in one of the explosions. Most of the people remaining behind are Diego's soldiers and security.

A hand grabs the edge of the tablecloth in front of me, and the head of one of the guards appears under the table. He grabs me by the hair, dragging me out, just as Nana Guadalupe presses her gun to his temple and fires. Blood and brain matter explode all over my dress, but I don't have the time to dwell on it because another set of hands seize my ankle and tugs me back. I grab onto the table's leg and turn to see Diego's furious face.

"Come here, bitch!" he snarls, pulling on my leg.

I aim the gun at his chest and let the bullet fly, but it hits his shoulder, which only enrages him more. He yanks on my leg again, and the gun slips from my hand.

My heart skips and my breathing stops. Cold sweat breaks across my forehead. My eyes go wide as Diego levels his gun on me.

Suddenly, a huge mass of something black smashes into Diego's side and the bullet meant for me explodes into the overturned chair, missing me by inches, but raining debris all around. I gape at the beast that holds Diego's neck in her jaws, listening to the strange gurgling sounds coming from the throat of the soon-to-be-dead man.

"Mimi?"

The dog turns its head toward me without letting go of its

prey, shakes her head, and Diego's bones break with a crunching sound. A long whistle reaches my ears, and Mimi's head immediately snaps to the side. She lets out a low growl and dashes after a soldier who's running away. I watch with wide eyes as she jumps on his back, throwing him to the ground. Blood sprays everywhere as Mimi sinks her canines into the back of the man's neck.

The whooshing sound keeps piercing the air every couple of seconds. Another explosion booms, followed by one more, and the left side of the house where the kitchen used to be collapses, a cloud of dust envelops everything around.

The cocking of a gun sounds behind me, and I turn to see Nana Guadalupe aiming at another soldier. She fires but misses. The man begins to raise his firearm but stills in mid-motion and falls to his knees, revealing a black-clad figure standing several yards away, holding a gun. I blink, then stare, taking in his tactical pants and the assortment of weapons strapped around his legs. I let my eyes travel up over the bulletproof vest and black shirt to lock on his face, camouflaged with military paint. I can't see his features clearly, but I'd recognize his pale hair anywhere.

"Sergei," I whisper, and tears streak down my face. He came for me.

"Your Russian is even more handsome all geared up," Nana Guadalupe mumbles next to me.

"What?" I ask, not moving my eyes off Sergei as he runs toward a parked car where two more soldiers are hiding.

"Last night, when I was taking dinner to Diego's soldiers in the barracks, he jumped out of the bushes. I almost had a heart attack."

"You knew what he was planning? Why didn't you say anything?"

Sergei stops, shoots one of the soldiers, then continues running while jumping over dead bodies on the ground.

"He said it was a surprise." She chuckles. "I think it's romantic."

"Romantic?" I take in the crumbling walls of my childhood home, then scan the lawn covered with blood and dead bodies, halting at the two outer buildings just off to the side. Or . . . what was left of them.

A loud bark reaches me, and I snap my head back to Sergei, who has almost reached the car where Mimi is attacking the remaining soldier. There's another man ducked behind the pile of debris, thirty or so feet from Sergei. He's clutching a rifle in his hand, and as I watch, he raises the weapon. I grab my gun from the ground, aim, and send all the bullets I have left at the soldier. Two hit him in the chest, and he topples over. Nana, too, cocks her gun and fires three more bullets that way.

"Just in case," she comments.

When I look back at Sergei, he's standing over the body of the last soldier, blood dripping from a long knife in his hand, talking into his headpiece. He throws a look at the man Nana and I just shot, then turns toward us and raises his thumb. Yeah, he might be a little whacky, but I love him anyway.

The rumble of an engine nears, and a couple of seconds later, a car stops on the driveway, and Felix's head pokes out of the window.

"Let's go!" he shouts.

I take Nana's hand in mine, and we run to the car.

Sergei

Angelina pushes her nana onto the passenger seat, but I can't make a move to join them yet. There could still be someone around, and I plan on eliminating them before they even think about becoming a threat to my girl. I'm not sure how many of Diego's men I killed in the last twenty minutes. Somewhere between thirty and forty based on the rough count.

I wasn't thinking too clearly, and don't even recall how I ended half of them. I was scared shitless that someone may hurt Angelina if I wasn't fast enough. It was adrenaline, instinct, and muscle memory, but I'm fairly certain I got all of the hostiles. Mimi took care of a few. And I think Angelina's nana offed at least three. It sucks that I didn't get the opportunity to kill Diego myself, but having his throat torn out must have been an extremely unpleasant way to die. That fact makes me really happy.

Angelina shuts the door after Guadalupe, but instead of getting inside the car, she turns to face me and just stares at me with her hand covering her mouth. Her fancy dress is torn up in a few places, and blood has been splattered over most of it, but it's nothing compared to what I probably look like. I should have let Guadalupe tell her about my plan and keep Angelina inside. It's possible she's even more scared of me now. Quickly, I hide my hand that's still holding the knife I used to kill the last man behind my back. I don't dare approach her because I don't think I could stomach it if she flinches away from me. If there is one thing I can't bear, it's Angelina being afraid of me. When she lowers her hand I see she's crying, and something inside of me falls to pieces.

I step back.

Felix can take them to a safe place and come back for me later. I won't make her endure my presence or distress her any more than necessary. Maybe I should go around and check if any of the motherfuckers are still alive and correct that mishap. Yes, I'll do that. I will my eyes away from Angelina and head to the nearest body when I hear her call my name. I turn around, and my eyes widen as she bolts toward me on bare feet, clutching the skirt of her ruined dress in her hands.

"Sergei!" she calls again, jumps over a dead soldier, and leaps into my arms. "You came for me."

"Of course, I came for you," I say and kiss her like my life depends on it. "I will always come for you, baby."

Angelina squeezes her arms around my neck and her legs tighten around my waist. "You owe me a house."

"Yeah, sorry about that. I got a little carried away."

"A little?" She snorts and buries her face in the crook of my neck. "I thought I would never see you again."

"Why didn't you say anything? I would have taken care of Diego for you, baby."

"He told me he would kill you if I didn't come back." She presses her palms on my cheeks and looks into my eyes. "I could never risk your life. I don't think I would ever forgive myself if something happened to you because of me."

"Well, I'm sure no one would miss me and my shit."

"Do not say that!" She squeezes my face. "Don't you dare say that ever again! Felix would miss you. Mimi. Your brother."

"Oh, Roman probably would throw a party."

"That's not true, and you know it." She leans forward,

pressing her lips to mine, then pulls back to look me in the eyes. "I would miss you."

My body goes stone-still. "Why?"

"Because I'm in love with you," she whispers and kisses me again.

When she pulls back, I search her face. "I thought you were scared of me. You said so in the note you left."

"I've never been scared of you, Sergei. What I feared was that you might come after me and end up dead. I'm so sorry for hurting you, baby."

"So . . . you're coming back? With me?"

"If you have nothing against that plan, yes."

I look down into her eyes and crush her to me. "Marry me," I blurt out.

Angelina blinks, glances around us where at least twenty bodies are scattered, then stares back at me. "You really know how to pick the time and place, big guy."

"Will you marry me?"

I think my heart stops beating while I watch her with eyes glued to her lips, waiting for her answer.

"Of course, I will." She grins and kisses me.

Suddenly, a loud honk comes from the direction of the driveway and Angelina tenses in my arms. Grinding my teeth, I look at the car where Felix keeps pressing on the horn.

"I'm going to kill him," I bite out. The old bat just ruined my marriage proposal.

"Will you two lovesick idiots come here already so we can leave?" Felix yells with his head out the window.

"You're dead, Albert!" I say as I carry Angelina to the car.

"We'll all be dead if we don't leave right now! I'm sure that half of Mexico's police force and firemen are on their way here. Along with a seismic team, because you decided to rearrange the fucking continent with your explosions!"

"Just shut the fuck up and drive."

I open the back door and whistle for Mimi to get inside, then sit in the rear, still holding Angelina in my arms. The moment Felix starts the car, I press my face into her hair and inhale her scent.

"I thought I was going to lose my mind when you left," I mumble next to her ear.

"I'm so sorry. I promise I'm going to make up for it as soon as we get home."

"Yeah, about that . . . we'll be staying in a hotel for a week or two," I say and lightly bite the side of her neck.

"In a hotel?"

"The house is being redecorated."

"Oh? Why?"

"Sergei smashed everything that wasn't attached to a wall when you left, that's why," Felix throws over his shoulder.

"Will you shut up already?" I snap. "She may change her mind and run away if you keep babbling on about how deranged I am."

Angelina's hand cups my cheek and turns my head toward her. "What did I tell you? You will stop saying stuff like that. Okay?" She leans in and kisses me. "There's nothing wrong with you, baby."

I squeeze her to me and bury my nose in her hair again, and for the first time in years, I feel like I might be okay.

EPILOGUE

One month later

"HEY, HOW ABOUT WE ORDER SOME BLINDS FOR the windows downstairs?" I ask as I enter the bedroom. "We could also . . ."

Dressed only in sweatpants, Sergei is sitting on the bed and staring at the wall in front of him, his body still and eyes vacant. Shit. He hasn't zoned out once since we got back from Mexico. I leave the stack of clean towels I'm carrying and slowly approach the bed.

"Hey, baby." I stand between his legs and wrap my arms around his neck. "I was thinking, maybe we could paint the living room pink. That girly, pastel shade, you know?"

He doesn't move a muscle. Leaning in, I press my lips to his and trail kisses from his mouth, up his cheek to his forehead, then continue down his nose until I reach his mouth again. This time, his lips move slightly, responding to my kiss.

"Felix and Nana Guadalupe took Mimi out for a walk," I

ramble as I press my palms to his chest and push on it lightly until he lies down on the bed. "I think something is going on between those two. They have been spending a lot of time together. Do you think Felix is cheating on Marlene with my nana?"

"He and Marlene broke up last weekend," Sergei says and places his hand on my hip. He's still away, but he's coming back slowly.

"We should use this time alone. What do you think?" I straddle his waist and bend to place a kiss at the center of his chest. "I can massage you with my oils after if you want."

"No, thank you."

I look down to find him staring up at me, but his eyes are still unfocused. Damn, this is a bad one. Tugging the waistband of his sweats, I slide them off along with his boxer briefs as I kneel before him, then I take his hardening cock in my hand, lean in, and suck on the tip. It twitches hardens more in my hand, and I can't help but smile. Even zoned out, he still responds to me. I run my tongue along the underside of his hard cock. I take him fully in my mouth and suck. I do these same movements a few more times before crawling back up his body and placing my nose to his when I notice he hasn't fully come back to me.

"Will you make love to me, baby?" I trace the tip of my finger down his nose. "Please."

Sergei's hands come to the small of my back, then glide up along my spine, lifting my shirt with them. He takes the hem between his fingers, and in the next moment, the sound of fabric being torn fills the room. Smiling, I take the ruined shirt off, do the same with my shorts and panties, and straddle him again, positioning myself above his cock.

"I love you," I whisper.

Sergei blinks, then meets my gaze, his light eyes filled with desire. He grabs onto my hips, slamming me down on his cock, and I gasp.

"I fell asleep." He pulls me onto his chest, then rolls us until he is on top of me. "I dreamed about Diego dragging you back to Mexico."

His hand slides into the hair at my nape, gripping it, while his cock slides out. I grab his shoulders, pulling at him and arching my back, trying to get him inside me again, but Sergei just smirks and moves his free hand to my pussy, teasing my clit.

"What are you doing?" I moan.

"Playing." His hand disappears, and his cock slides inside. He drives into me twice, then pulls out again. His finger replaces his cock.

A growl filled with frustration and need leaves my lips. "Sergei!"

"Yes, baby?"

"I need you," I choke out. "Inside. Now."

"How much?" The finger in my pussy curls and hits a spot that has my body shivering. Then the finger vanishes, making me want to scream. I'm so close. If he continues to torture me, I'm going to lose my mind.

He pinches my clit, then slides his finger back inside. "I asked, how much, Angelina."

"I'm going to kill you," I whisper in his ear, move my mouth to his shoulder and bite him. Hard.

A low growling sound leaves Sergei's lips as he thrusts into me, burying his cock to the hilt. His hand drifts down my leg until it reaches my knee.

"You little cheat." He moves my leg up and to the side, opening me wider.

I smile, then moan as he starts pounding into me and clutch at his shoulders, trying to keep myself from sliding up the bed. It doesn't quite work, so I brace my hands against the headboard and pant as his hips jackhammer me into a mattress. He is so big it hurts a little, but it's the good kind of pain. One that reminds me he's here, both mentally and physically. As orgasmic tremors rock my body, my eyes drift shut, but a heartbeat later, Sergei grabs the back of my neck.

"Look at me," he barks while going completely rigid, his cock swelling impossibly more as he finds his own release.

I gasp and open my eyes. Placing my palm on his cheek, I peer into his light depths. "Always," I whisper.

Angelina

Four years later

"Mommy."

I look up from the juice I'm squeezing and smile when my eyes land on our three-year-old son, who's clutching Mimi around the neck. With my dark hair and Sergei's light eyes, he's the perfect mix of both of us. "What is it, Sasha?"

"Daddy's sleeping awake again," he says.

I leave the orange on the counter and cross the kitchen to crouch in front of him. "Did you try giving him a kiss to wake him up?"

"No."

"Let's go do it together, then. Yes?"

"Okay." He takes my hand and leads me to the living room.

Sergei is standing in front of the window, motionless, staring at something outside. I lift our boy in my arms and come to stand in front of my husband.

"Ready?" I ask, and Sasha nods eagerly. "Okay, hold tight, just in case."

As I lean our son toward his dad, he wraps his little arms around Sergei's neck and places a kiss on his cheek. Sergei's hands shoot out instantly, seizing the boy around the waist and pulling Sasha tightly to his chest.

"Sorry." Sergei bends to place a kiss on my lips. "How long?"

"No more than five minutes," I say into his mouth. "You're doing great, baby."

Sergei's episodes have diminished significantly over the last couple of years. This one was the first in the past three or four months. They don't last for hours anymore, and it's easier for him to snap out of them.

"When are Albert and Guadalupe arriving?"

"Why do you keep calling him that?" I laugh. "He hasn't lived here in three years."

Sergei smirks. "Because it pisses him off. Crazy old bat. Did you hear what he bought Guadalupe for their anniversary?"

"Nope."

"A shotgun."

"Classy. I'm sure she'll love it. When do they ..." My eyes snag on the TV behind Sergei that's showing breaking news. "Whoa. Did you see this?"

I grab the remote and turn up the volume, staring at the live video of the aerial view of what looks like the aftermath of a devastating fire. The news ticker at the bottom of the screen says it's happening in the New York area. There's no way to tell what the structure was before the fire, only the general shape remains. The scene changes to images of a man and a woman who have been presumed dead in the fire. The man looks to be in late thirties, handsome, wearing a suit. He seems like a businessman. I shift my gaze to the other photo. The text under it says the woman is twenty-three, but the black pantsuit she's wearing, aloof expression, and stern hairstyle make her look older. The news anchor keeps talking in the background, but I don't catch what she says because Sergei bursts out laughing next to me.

"I knew it." He snorts and shakes his head. "Someone must have really pissed off the antisocial motherfucker."

I stare at him, confused. "What are you talking about?"

"That." He points at the TV screen, which is once again showing the destruction caused by the fire. "See how evenly and thoroughly the building is burned down? That's extremely hard to achieve. I only know one person who can pull it off." He laughs again. "Albert is going to lose it when I tell him Az is alive."

"The guy from your unit? The one who disappeared?"

"Yup." He places a kiss on Sasha's cheek, then places his hand at the small of my back, right over my tattoo and pulls me into his side.

I meant what I said all those years ago, when I agreed to having 'Prinadlezhit Sergeyu Belovu' tattooed on me, and was both surprised and amused when Sergei asked the tattoo artist to replicate the words on him too, replacing his name for mine.

There's a sound of approaching steps, and I look over my shoulder to see Felix and Nana walking into the room. Felix looks up at the TV, then stops abruptly.

"I'm going to fucking kill him," he snaps, shaking his head while glaring at the screen. "He promised he would stay low. Does this look like staying low to you?"

"You tricky old ass," Sergei barks, staring at Felix. "You knew Az was alive?"

"Knew?" Felix raises an eyebrow. "How exactly did you think he managed to disappear and stay under the government's radar?"

"Do you know his real name?"

"Of course, I do."

"What is it?" Sergei asks.

Felix just smiles. "Wouldn't you like to know?" He looks back at the TV. "I wonder what rattled his cage so much that he resurfaced after eight years."

The End

Dear reader,

Thanks so much for reading Sergei's story! I hope you'll consider leaving a review, letting the other readers know what you thought of Hidden Truths. Even if it's just one short sentence, it makes a huge difference. Reviews help authors find new readers, and help other readers find new books to love!

If you want to read more of my books, check out my website, or my author page on Amazon, and stay up to date by following me on TikTok (@author_neva_altaj).

The next book in the series is Ruined Secrets, which follows Luca Rossi (Sergei's gun supplier) and Isabella (the granddaughter of the don of the Chicago branch of La Cosa Nostra). This is an arranged marriage, age gap story (Luca is 35, Isabella is 19).

And, in case you were wondering about that last scene in the epilogue :D—yes, it was a teaser for one of the future books, which will feature Az, Sergei's friend from the Z.E.R.O. unit. It will probably be book #7 in the series.

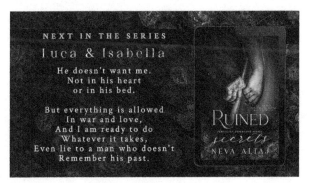

NEXT IN THE SERIES
Luca & Isabella

He doesn't want me.
Not in his heart
or in his bed.

But everything is allowed
In war and love,
And I am ready to do
Whatever it takes,
Even lie to a man who doesn't
Remember his past.

RUINED
secrets
NEVA ALTAJ

Acknowledgments

In my opinion, writing a book is the easiest part of the job. The harder tasks come after, and my books wouldn't be half they are if it weren't for the people who worked with me to help me bring my stories to life.

The person whom I need to thank the most is my editor. Thank you, Susan! I have no idea what I would have done without you. <3 I'm sorry for all the missing commas, thousands of "sighs," "gasps," and "slams" you had to swap with other words, as well as grammar mistakes you keep correcting (and explaining) only for me to continue making them again and again. I'm trying, I swear! Susan is also my alpha reader who goes over the first drafts, and believe me, reading that shit is painful. LOL. Thank you for dealing with that, too. <3

A big thank you to my proofreaders, Andie, Mich, and Yvette, who caught all the typos and provided great advice for improvement.

A huge thank you to my personal assistant, Caitlen, who does all the heavy lifting as far as book launches are concerned. If it wasn't for her, I probably wouldn't have time to write. I'd be too immersed in handling ARCs, book mail, blog tours, and politely rejecting people who offer to do paid reviews (man, I had no idea there are so many!). Thank you for everything.

And of course, a big thank you to Shaima, who beta-read Sergei's story and gave amazing guidelines and suggestions for improving the book. <3

A most heartfelt thank you goes out to my readers, who

took a chance on a debut author and showed so much love and support, encouraging me to keep writing. Thank you for every review, share, Instagram, and TikTok post because you have no idea how powerful a motivator it is to see that people like your stories. The Perfectly Imperfect world was originally conceived as a five-book series, but after receiving so much positive feedback, I had to keep writing. I'm not sure how many books there will be when I'm done, but I'm planning at least three additional stories after Stolen Touches, book 5 of the series.

I love you! <3

ABOUT THE
author

Neva Altaj writes steamy contemporary mafia romance about damaged antiheroes and strong heroines who fall for them. She has a soft spot for crazy jealous, possessive alphas who are willing to burn the world to the ground for their woman. Her stories are full of heat and unexpected turns, and a happily-ever-after is guaranteed every time.

Neva loves to hear from her readers,
so feel free to reach out:

Website: www.neva-altaj.com
Facebook: @neva.altaj
TikTok: @author_neva_altaj
Instagram: @neva_altaj
Goodreads: www.goodreads.com/Neva_Altaj

Made in the USA
Monee, IL
25 September 2023

43400646R00149